THE ROUNDERS

THE ROUNDERS

Max Evans

University of New Mexico Press ⑤ Albuquerque

© 2010 by Max Evans
All rights reserved. Published 2010
Printed in the United States of America
16 15 14 13 12 11 10   1 2 3 4 5 6 7

Library of Congress Cataloging-in-Publication Data
Evans, Max, 1924–
  The rounders / Max Evans.
      p. cm.
  ISBN 978-0-8263-4913-2 (pbk. : alk. paper)
  I. Title.
  PS3555.V23R68 2010
  813'.54—dc22
              2010011524

A **FOREWORD** TO REVEAL
HOW A SMALL BOOK COULD LEAD TO KNOWING AND ADVENTURING WITH MANY HOLLYWOOD STARS AND DIRECTORS

How in the world of insanity and wonder could it all happen? Fifty very long years ago, I would not have believed it possible—but here it is in my battered old hands, the fiftieth anniversary edition of *The Rounders*. This little book would change the direction of my life—from the first book signing until now. Throughout those fifty years, I met scores of people in all walks of life. Some I talked to for five minutes, others would become lifelong friends. It led me to deep involvement in the world of films and television, where I met and became close friends with many of the most talented and famous actors, producers, and directors.

I wrote *The Rounders* because I had to. I had to because I had a story banging around in my head that I just had to put on paper; I had to in order to support my wife, Pat, and our twin girls, Charlotte and Sheryl . . . and . . . I had to because due to the failure of a mining venture I was $86,000 in debt and needed a miracle to pay it off. Desperation is a great motivator.

I wasn't totally new at the writing game, having already had two books (a collection of short stories and a biography, *Long John*

Dunn of Taos) and dozens of magazine articles published. None had even come close to paying any big debts, but *this* one was going to be different. Right?

I began work on the book that would change my entire life (and that of my wife and daughters) by following the old "write-what-you-know-about" adage. I had all the true, firsthand experience it would take to do this novel.

I was about six years old when I started my early learning about "cowboying" by herding a small bunch of cows for a widowed aunt who needed milk for her five young daughters in Humble City, New Mexico (a tiny town my dad founded just before the great crash in 1929). But naturally, I sure didn't know it would ever lead to anything close to my writing *The Rounders*. Since this was in the depths of a great drought and the Depression of the 1930s, it kept me scheming daily and scrounging to the limit to keep these cows fed and producing when there was so little for them to eat, but responsibility helped create an ever-present survival instinct in me. I told of this in detail in my book *For the Love of a Horse* (UNM Press, 2007).

When I was around ten years old my cowboy education advanced as I was taught, by the few local ranchers who still had cattle, how to throw a calf, vaccinate, de-horn, earmark, and brand it. I was even allowed to head-or-heel and drag a calf to the fire. I strutted as proud as any twenty-year-old.

Three months from my being twelve years old, my parents decided to leave the depression-and-drought-destroyed town of Humble City and move to Andrews, just across the New Mexico border in West Texas. They allowed me to fulfill a dream and go to the mountains and mesas of north central New Mexico to work on a ranch, the Rafter EY, where I was certain my childhood wishes and visions of meeting real Indians, Latinos, and other working cowboys would come true. My romanticism of this magnificent landscape was fulfilled, but so was a sore butt from countless miles in the saddle looking after cattle, trying to ride bucking horses, gathering wild steers, and the daywork I did on loan-out to other ranchers. Digging postholes and stringing barbwire fences, shoveling hard layers of manure out of barns, and breaking ice on tanks so the cattle could water in the winter produced other sore muscles and lots of blistered hands before the calluses came. Soon the brandings—even with all their hard work—became vacations because I had perfected the art of heeling calves. I grew to love cowboying and all the people I worked with.

Fortunately, my mother taught me to read long before I started school. I loved books and reading. They were filled with the same kind of adventures I wanted to experience. On a shelf at the Rafter EY ranch I discovered a small set of Balzac novels and have devoured the words of the little potbellied Frenchman ever since. *The Rounders* would be about as far removed from his style as possible, but the obsession with Balzac's books led me to read the finest works the writers of the world could produce. Luck? I guess.

Anyway, I managed all this and even got some schooling, and by luck again owned my own small ranch over in far northeast New Mexico by the time I was seventeen. Although it was watered by springs and had good grama and buffalo grass, there just wasn't enough acreage to make a living. To hold it together, I had to work out at day labor.

I worked some for the Cross L near the Colorado border, a few times on the huge T. O. headquartered near Raton, and often on large neighboring ranches like those owned by A. D. Weatherly and Ferrol Smith. I even broke out a couple strings of horses for the Jones Brothers. I was determined to get more land, but soon discovered the big powers surrounding me weren't going to sell an acre. They were just waiting to get mine.

This situation, which seemed unfeasible at the time, led to many real scenes in *The Rounders*. My brain must have turned to half-scrambled eggs considering all the foolish things I would get involved with later.

Then, of course, the greatest of all wars, World War II, came upon the entire globe, including mine. Where I lived then there was no mail delivery, no electricity, no newspapers, no telephones, no radios. I heard secondhand about this war from the few and far-scattered neighbors I encountered about whose sons or daughters were going to faraway lands to fight. I couldn't take this news, so I went off to join that mess as well.

Of course, since I had spent my days making a living on horseback, naturally the Army put me in the *walking* Infantry. I was pretty good at walking and shooting and by a miracle wasn't made a sniper. After landing at Omaha on D-1 and fighting in three major battles and absorbing the impact of a 500-pound railroad shell, I finally made it back to the ranch, but found my perspective took a turn away from ranching. I began to realize that life on the ranch wasn't going to happen for me at this time. I didn't want to borrow money to restock my herd when I could make a deal with the Jones boys to run their cattle on my outfit.

Maybe art was what I should pursue next. I always liked to draw and enjoyed looking at paintings. It seemed to be the answer. For now anyway.

So, I commuted—when I could—to Amarillo, Texas, to study art with Ida Strawn Baker, an internationally recognized artist who was temporarily in Amarillo to settle an estate. The result of this temporary study was my falling just as deeply in love with fine paintings as I had with fine books.

This too was doomed to end with reality here in the heart of pure cow country, because I knew only one other person living here who really cared about art at all—Luz Martínez, who worked for the railroad. He was taking a correspondence course in art. We became close friends. But our art interests made us feel a little weird and outcast.

I sold the ranch and moved fourteen miles into Des Moines, where I bought 120 acres with two windmills and two houses on it. Luz quit the railroad and we started drawing and painting in one of the houses. For a while I stayed. At that time there seemed to be no future in my newfound art career in Des Moines, so I moved to Taos, where all the real artists lived, fully intending to become rich and famous in less than two years, but I became broke and infamous in less time than that. Later, Luz followed and had enough sense to turn his studies towards making carved furniture and Santos.

Then I met my mentor, the great Potawatomie Indian artist Woody Crumbo (see the 2009 book distributed by the University of Oklahoma Press entitled *Uprising—Woody Crumbo's Art*, by Robert Perry). Crumbo was a great teacher. I learned fast from him. Soon

I was selling paintings, a few magazine articles, and a few short stories for small sums. I could feed my new bride, Pat, most of the time. She had lived in Taos as a child and knew some of the old Taos masters and had modeled for a few of them. She had the right "savvy" for a new and crazy artist.

About five years into this Crumbo friendship, Woody and I went into the mining business. That is the only world crazier than cowboying and the arts. We made a go of the mining business because of the excitement of the uranium boom. We had blocked out a lot of copper and contracted with Molybdenum Corporation of America to reconstruct part of their mill to process part of our production—150 tons a day. In the meantime we started shipping ore to El Paso at the AS & R smelter. We were rich. I say it again, we were rich. We could have sold out for many millions at that time.

Then it happened—the price of copper started down. We spent all we had trying to hold it together hoping for a return to the profitable prices. But the price dropped in half in ninety days.

A year before the disaster, Dan Hurley, a fine and experienced geologist, explained with a graph on a large piece of paper that major copper companies always existed in a nine-year arc of up and down, up and down. During the up times they put away funds to carry them through the down times. With the enthusiasm of foxhunting hounds, we ignored his advice and went right on spending money and having fun. There it was again—those two dreaded words—flat broke.

I went "kersplat" right through the floor. I owed $86,000—which was about like suddenly being worth $400,000-below-nothing in today's terms.

Crumbo soon took a job running the El Paso Museum of Fine Arts, while I stayed in Taos staring at the mountain by that name. I had long ago sold all my paintings. It would take me a year, at least, to paint enough for a show, and my magazine stories paid too little. Being a proven mathematical idiot, I could still reason that I would never pay off the $86,000 debt before my hundredth birthday. I talked it over with Pat and decided I should take a crack at writing. So it was confirmed—I'd write a novel. *The Rounders* was about to begin.

What would my subject matter be? Everyone says, "Write what you know." I knew about a lot of things by now, but I didn't care to go through the battles of France, Belgium, and Germany. The mining was still too close and painful for me to have a perspective on it. I thought about Jack London, who I read early on. I knew the hunting of animals for survival. I had read Will James and thought his words and drawings were first-rate. Wait a minute, he had only told half the story of working cowboys of the time. He had mostly left out how they acted and reacted on their trips to town.

There it was. I'd tell the whole deal, especially the camaraderie they had to develop in order to survive their long stints on the lonesome land and their usually very brief stays in town.

Now, it took a while for this short novel to get on paper. Our own survival was necessary while the book was being written. I traded in horses, antiques, santos, old lumber, and countless other things while working on the book. It was finally finished. Hooray and hallelujah. Rich again. Soon—as soon as I could find a publisher to buy it.

I had been introduced to one of the world's great agencies by a woman who once worked for Russell & Volkening in New York. She read the manuscript and said they would just love it. They did. I started counting the money in my feeble mind and figuring who would get paid first, and all that ridiculous nonsense.

A whole new world with a different set of rules was about to open up.

Henry Volkening was world famous for holding martini lunches with the heads of great publishing houses and selling them before the fourth drink. This time it was different for him. *The Rounders* was praised highly by the editors in chief of eleven great houses. All turned it down with this same statement in different words "We love it. The book is a hilarious western and feels real. But . . . we don't have an audience or a category for that."

It began to look as if the BIG debt would have to wait a while longer, when the letter came from the editor in chief of Macmillan (the largest publisher in the world at the time). They bought it. I got a small advance, but it seemed huge to me.

In the fifties and sixties the best New York literary agencies were allowed to submit manuscripts directly to MGM well in advance of their publication. The manuscripts were placed on a large "slush table." Directors could search for an *early look* at stories. That's where Burt Kennedy discovered *The Rounders*. Burt Kennedy had written the six best screenplays for Randolph Scott, including *Seven Men from Now*, thought by most critics to be Scott's best, saving his career. Kennedy had also directed some good TV shows and one feature. So he was listened to.

Sometimes the phone rings and it's real important. I got that call from Fess Parker, the movie actor who had become the number one star in the world because of Disney's Davy Crockett films. Burt Kennedy had taken *The Rounders* to Parker, who was looking for a project, and Fess loved it. He asked Pat and me to come to California. We could stay with him and his wife in their mansion in Santa Barbara and put *The Rounders* together. The action was on, and it was a marvelous adventure.

We made the deal and returned to Taos. In a few weeks a call came inviting us and our little twins to return to Santa Barbara, stay in the Parkers' guesthouse, and get on with a script and all that whipped-cream stuff.

Oh, yes, the big debt was shrinking—gradually.

It is amazing how much talk and how many trips take place before a script is done, or a movie is made. And I will say this: on my trips to Hollywood with Ol' Fess I was wined and dined just like the rest of the stars. Slowly I became acquainted with people in show business who would become lifelong friends.

Now during our meetings in Hollywood with stars, producers, agents, and money managers and on and on, something had taken place I was not aware of. Burt Kennedy was out of the picture and a man I had only heard of remotely, but whose original films I loved, was suddenly going to be the director—William Wellman. He had done such films as *The High and The Mighty* (John Wayne), *The Ox-Bow Incident* (Henry Fonda), and *Track of the Cat* (Robert Mitchum). He was a legend among the legendary. He had retired, and no amount of cajoling or offers of money had changed his mind until *The Rounders*.

Wellman went to work daily on *The Rounders* script with Tom

Blackburn—Fess Parker's writer on the Davy Crockett films. I was highly honored by this, and almost everyone I met was just as impressed. Actually, I was only aware of this later. I was naive, and just thought *What a lot of nice people!*

Everyone seemed so excited. Enthusiasm was high. Hollywood and films do that to people.

I did wonder what had become of Burt Kennedy and Slim Pickens, who Fess insisted I talk to on the phone several times about the handling of the horse, Old Fooler, and other things I was vague about. We met over and over with Wellman and Blackburn. It was the talk of the western part of the "town."

The Rounders project had been verbally accepted for production by United Artists. We all met to close the deal. In the office at United Artists, Fess and Wellman disagreed on the casting, and just like it started, it was over. Wellman walked. It didn't bother me as much as it should have. Hell, I'd just stay here in Hollywood and make another deal. The property was hot, so it shouldn't take too long.

Pat and the twins went back to Taos. I checked into a small hotel for a while, then that great character actor, Morgan Woodward, graciously invited me to stay with him in his North Hollywood home. My funds were scant, to say the least, and this generosity allowed me to extend my mission.

The Hollywood bug had bitten. The money was excellent, the people were fun, and I felt that I couldn't quit until a deal on *The Rounders* was made, but I didn't stay too long. I decided to leave the dealings to my agent, and I went home to write another book, *The Hi Lo Country*.

In the next four years, I sold three options on *The Rounders*. None were renewed. Then Burt Kennedy came back into the corral and along with producer Richard Lyons was able to cast two of America's greatest stars, Henry Fonda and Glenn Ford. Two really terrific guys whose talent made dozens and dozens of films memorable. Those two unforgettable, fabulous females Sue Ann Langdon and Hope Holiday really stole the show. It also starred some of the best character actors ever known: Chill Wills, Warren Oates, Edgar Buchanan, Denver Pyle, and all the others, plus five roan horses to play one Old Fooler. The movie has now played on national TV several times annually for nearly fifty years.

It was made into a TV series for CBS starring John Wayne's son, Pat. This led me to know his father, John Wayne, and John's other son, Michael. Michael's company hired me to do a screenplay especially for the Duke. John Wayne was ill but nobody wanted to accept that he couldn't go on forever. He died very soon after the script was completed. He did get to read it and hoped to do it.

This, directly or indirectly, led me to become close, lifelong friends with director Sam Peckinpah (*The Wild Bunch*, *The Ballad of Cable Hogue*, *Straw Dogs*, and others).

I met Sam when my agent called and said the hot new director of *Ride the High Country* loved my new book, *The Hi Lo Country*. Now Sam wanted me to come to Hollywood. I didn't know who Sam Peckinpah was, but again took the bait.

We had lunch across from Warner Brothers in the valley at a popular movie hangout, The Polynesian. The meal lasted from noon until they threw us out at 2:00 a.m.

He bought an option on *Hi Lo* for pretty good money. It was announced in the trades and all over, and again people were seeking my company and had turned even nicer than ever.

It was much later, after endless options and trades with Sam Peckinpah, that I found out *The Rounders* was responsible for all of this. Sam had hired Joe Barnhard, a schoolmate from their youth, to be his story editor and confidante. Joe had discovered *The Round-ers* in the MGM slush pile, read it, loved it, and insisted Sam read it. He did, but too late. Burt Kennedy and Fess had already latched onto it. Sam was, to say the least, sort of insanely disappointed, so, when Joe found *The Hi Lo Country*, in manuscript form, on another "slush table" and recommended that Sam read it, he did so in one evening, called my agent, and we became close friends until his death almost a quarter of a century later.

Just before Sam left for Mexico to direct *Major Dundee* he called to invite us to stay in his Malibu house on Zuma Beach while he was gone. He said I could work on the book I was writing and we could all enjoy the peace and quiet of the ocean. As it turned out we had regular visits from Lee Marvin, who was one extremely entertaining person. He usually brought a friend or two to have a bigger audience. We never knew who would show up, and I will say many lifelong friendships were formed. Daytime was for work, evenings for great fun and even serious conversations. When *Major Dundee* was finished in Mexico we were prepared to go back to Taos the next day, but Sam said, "No. You have to stay until the kids' school starts." So we did, and everything escalated.

Sam is now a cult director all over the world because of *The Wild Bunch* and many more classic films. During Sam's lifetime, he wasn't able to get a single one of my books made into a film, but he sure as hell used parts of them—and bragged proudly to me about doing it. At one time or the other he optioned many of my books: *The Hi Lo Country*, *My Pardner*, *The Great Wedding*, *Big Shad's Bridge*, and even *The One Eyed Sky*. Peckinpah once told Allen Keller, an extra, a stuntman, and mainly a bodyguard, that he was going to buy every book of mine he could and if he couldn't get them made he would nail them up on the wall so no one else could make them. But he didn't, and all the options lapsed many years ago on the ones he had been able to acquire.

It seems just as much a fantasy as ever that this all came about because of a little book written in desperation to feed my family and pay off a mining debt.

Back in Taos, a few months after our Malibu stay, various scriptwriting deals kept coming. The pay was very good, but the separations from my family weren't. The solution was to move to California for a full school year. We rented a fully furnished house in Studio City. We met lots of new people who became lifelong friends, and cemented old friendships even further, and weekends at Sam's were almost mandatory. His greatest pleasure was to barbecue something—all day.

L. Q. Jones heard Martin Scorsese say he was interested in doing something western. L. Q. gave him *The Hi Lo Country*. The legendary Scorsese produced it, hiring noted British director Stephen Frears to add the magic. The 1998 film starred Woody Harrelson, Patricia Arquette, Billy Crudup, Sam Elliott, James Gammon, and Penelope Cruz. It was her first American film. Cruz received rave reviews for that featured role in *Hi Lo*. She has become an internationally known star and Oscar winner. She is a fine lady who deserves all these accolades and more, but I'll bet a good quarter horse against a three-legged goat she has no idea that this all started way back there with a little tragicomedy called *The Rounders*.

The Rounders was like magic—doors sprang open and deals were made, all resulting in business associations and/or friendships created by this book.

Some more movie and TV people were of great importance in our lives: directors Tommy Gries (*Will Penny*), Bernie Kowalski (*Krakatoa: East of Java, Baretta*), and director/writer David Peckinpah (Sam's nephew) (*Silk Stalkings, Beauty and the Beast*); two singer/actors with satin-smooth voices, Rex Allen and Robert Goulet; dear family friends, writer Jeb Rosebrook (*Junior Bonner, I Will Fight No More Forever*) and his wife Dorothy, and Em and Josh Bryant (*M*A*S*H, Into The West*). Brian Keith (*The Westerner*, the TV series *Family Affair*, as well as countless films and Broadway productions) was a very special friend. We were in close contact through letters and phone calls for as long as he lived. Other great friends included character actor Morgan Woodward (*Cool Hand Luke* and lots of westerns; he played more lead heavies in *Gunsmoke* than any other actor); James Gammon (many, many films, including *The Hi Lo Country* and *Bring Me the Head of Alfredo Garcia*); Pat Hingle (Broadway productions and scores of fine TV and film parts); and Emilio Fernández (*The Wild Bunch* and other sensitive performances). Other marvelous character actors that glue a film together, such as L. Q. Jones, Strother Martin, and Bo Hopkins, and stars Ricardo Montalban and Charlton Heston, were among countless others I had friendships and dealings with. I even did some script work for Burt Lancaster. That was a hell of an adventure novel all by itself.

Because of the "little book," we became fine friends of David Dortort (producer of *Bonanza, High Chaparral*, and more) and his wife, Rose. That great film-and-book critic and entertainment editor for the *L. A. Times*, Charles Champlin, is another great friend who is still enjoying many accolades. Also, that dear man John Sinor, syndicated columnist for the *San Diego Evening Tribune* for many years, was more fun than a Mel Brooks comedy. Two others are Buster Keaton (thought by most critics to be America's greatest comic) and Walon Green, author of *The Wild Bunch*, *The Border*, and *Hi Lo Country*, and producer of countless successful television series.

The list goes on and on, but it does hurt to even start trying to count those wonderful, entertaining, unforgettable people since I have outlived most of them.

I've been lucky to have a family that put up with all my often wild and foolish adventures. I was lucky as a child and as a young man to have cowboyed in Lea County, Glorieta Mesa, environs south of Santa Fe, and all over northeastern New Mexico, in the land that I call the Hi Lo Country in books, films, and in reality.

I have to confess that it does my old heart good to hear again from other old cowboys who laughingly tell me that they actually once owned a horse just like Old Fooler. And then for decades their sons, daughters, and grandchildren have related to me how their parents and grandparents had seen the film and/or read the book so many times they'd lost count. I'm proud to say that it has shown at least three times on television this year and been read by the same number because I received calls on both, in different months, from different people, and they're still laughing.

My greatest moment of pride for this little work might surprise some. Back in the late sixties suddenly I got requests from several universities to donate my original manuscripts to their archives. At that point in my career, I hadn't even thought about this, but when the suggestion was made I knew I wanted to do it. The principal enticement was a tax deduction for the gift.

I thought about it for several days before deciding which archives to accept. The University of Texas at El Paso is as far west as you can get in Texas and just an arrow shot from the New Mexico border. Since I was born in Texas, but had lived most of my life in New Mexico, that seemed to be the ideal place—even though they had not been among the ones who had solicited my work.

The head of the university's English department was Dr. C. L. (Doc) Sonnichsen. He had been the unquestioned dean of Southwestern writers/historians for over a decade and had gone around talking up my first three novels all the time. So, I called him. I told him I wished to give my manuscripts and letters to UTEP's archive. He started laughing and said he'd be more than honored to take them, but they didn't have an archive.

I don't know how it happened but I blurted out, "Well, by God, you do now."

He laughed again, and when I told him *The Rounders*, *The Hi Lo Country*, and *The One Eyed Sky* original manuscripts would be the first gifts, he said, "It's high time. I'll send a student of mine to pick them up tomorrow." The student was Leon Metz, now an award-winning El Paso historian.

The UTEP archive has grown enormously since then. One patron who speeded up the building of the collection was the renowned El Pasoan Charles Leavell, international builder and close friend of Tom and Sarah Lea for over fifty years. He donated his papers and a million dollars to the library at UTEP that houses our rarities. Its large collection now includes papers from Dale Walker, José Cisneros, Leon Metz, letters of Tom Lea, and many more of true note. It is called the Sonnichsen Special Collections and *The Rounders* was the first manuscript in the chute.

In the late sixties I was a founding member of Governor David Cargo's New Mexico Film Commission, the first one ever formed in the United States. I was able to help with this because of *The Rounders* and all my numerous friends in Hollywood.

I went to Hollywood alone—and on my own dollar—and enlisted help from my agent and John Wayne's company Batjac Productions, Sam Peckinpah, Burt Kennedy, and others, resulting in a breakfast at the Beverly Hills Hotel with Governor Cargo and several members of the commission. Fifty-seven major Hollywood players attended. Cargo made a short, powerful speech, and they loved him.

Governor Cargo said we brought over a billion and a half dollars in filming to the state, mainly by showing producers its beauty and desolation at minimal expense. Movies are going stronger than ever in New Mexico now because of large financial incentives given to the film companies.

As I take a long look backward over the fifty-year span from the printing of my first novel, *The Rounders*, to my very last, *War and Music: A Medley of Love*, I see a huge kaleidoscope of events blending into one little truth. *The Rounders'* characters and one ol' outlawed horse have given deep cleansing laughter to millions of people from the elite to plain folks of the land like me.

It paid off in a lot of ways, including the big debt of $86,000. That's a blessing in surplus for one little lifetime.

—MAX EVANS

ONE

Jim Ed Love is a very funny name for a man who likes nothing better than to see a cowboy get what little brains he's got kicked out by a rawboned, walleyed, bucking, ground-stopping bronc. Just the same, that's the way he is. Me and Wrangler listened to the same old story we'd heard ever since we'd started working for Jim Ed and the JL outfit.

"Now, boys, this ain't goin' to be no trouble a tall. Half of them ponies is broke already. Just look at the blaze-face roan standin' there like a milk-pen calf. Why, I bet he's been rode a thousand miles, and all it'll take to gentle him down is one or two saddlin's."

I could see from where I was standing, with the sun square in my eyes, that there was healed-over spur marks in that old pony's shoulder. That could mean just one thing. Trouble. I had worked for outfits that gave spoiled horses like that one away just to keep from crippling up good cowboys.

"Now, boys, that roan has got the makin's of a real rope horse, and after you get the tallow melted a little I'll probably want him for the old lady and kids to ride," Jim Ed went on.

One thing for sure, there ain't nobody going to catch Jim Ed riding one of them broncs and taking a chance on getting his tailor-made western suit dirty. I don't know whether he is too smart or too clean for it. He's the cleanest feller I ever saw. Stays shaved all the time, keeps his sixty-dollar boots shined, and that shirt, stretched so tight across his big belly, is starched like a priest's collar. He wears a big gold chain across his big belly with a gold watch on it that must weigh as much as a baby calf. His hat is whiter than a scared bronc's eyeballs.

You don't never see him out among his cows unless he is there to count them and see how many pounds they have gained and how many dollars he can put in the bank come shipping time. He ain't no cowboy, this Jim Ed Love, but he is a cowman. He don't never overstock his pastures and he always has plenty of hay up when a blizzard strikes. He can dicker for six days and nights for one-fourth cent a pound more for his beef. He can get more work from and give less pay to a cowboy than anybody I ever saw. Like right now, for instance. We oughta know, because me and Wrangler started working for him down at one of his many ranches at Andrews and Big Lake, Texas. He's also got a big hay outfit in Colorado, but the Hi Lo ranch was his favorite. He was going to expect us to break horses and work cows both at the same time, either one of them plenty for one man.

Wrangler snorted through his little flat busted nose, and then before Jim Ed could see the grin on his face he ran out and fore-footed a two-year-old black. The pony hit the end of the rope, and Wrangler dug his heels in the dirt. That colt went up and over and down right smack dab on the back of his neck. While this was going on, I decided to rope the roan.

Well sir, he went trotting around the corral like a workhorse on a hot day. I rolled that loop out in front of him, and he stepped in it like one of them trick horses you see at a fancy rodeo. I jerked the slack out of the rope and braced for the spill. Hell, that old pony just stopped and stood there.

"See there, boys?" Jim Ed yelled. "Just like I said—gentle as a milk-pen calf."

I had to admit that the roan acted mighty gentle, and began to think maybe I was wrong. Well, Jim Ed turned and climbed over the corral and crawled in his pickup and drove off toward town, leaving me and Wrangler to our rat killing.

I decided to catch a heavy-quartered bay three-year-old before I worked on the roan. I forefooted him and spilled him several times. He came up kicking, falling, snorting, and raising hell until I set back on that rope and piled him again. He finally caught on to the fact that when the rope pulled tight, unpleasant things happened to him. Pretty soon he just stood there trembling, and rolling his eyes.

I turned him loose and then I took another whirl with the loop and fit it around his neck. This was something else. Now we went barreling around the corral with my boot heels plowing two uneven tracks in the dirt.

I yelled at Wrangler, "Ear him down, ear him down; the son of a bitch is settin' my heels afire!"

Wrangler came sailing in looking like a bowlegged hog crossed with a short-shanked bear. He finally got that ear in his mouth and held on till I got a hackamore on the bay's head. We snubbed him up to a big post out in the middle of the corral. While he was fighting his head and stretching his neck ragged against that stout cedar pole, I went over and earred a brown bronc for Wrangler. I turned the rest of the horses out so there wouldn't be so many to kick at us.

Now, I ain't never figured how that ugly short-legged little devil could get up on a bronc, much less ride him, but once Wrangler was in the saddle he stuck like he was nailed there. Now me, I like to take a little more time about it. While the bay and Wrangler went sailing around the corral, I tried to keep out of their way long enough to get me a gunnysack.

I yelled, "Wrangler, get down and tie that brown to the corral fence while I sack this bay out." Well, every time I rubbed that sack on him he fell back and kicked and pawed right straight up in the air. After a while he quit and stood spread-legged and trembling, just like he'd done with the rope.

It don't take a smart horse too long to catch on to what's right and what's wrong. Now take that roan . . . wait a minute. I'll get to that skunk-hearted bastard later. Anyway, I finally got the saddle blanket over that bay's back and then the saddle. He romped around a little bit, but when I jerked the cinch up he farted like an overloaded pack mule and started bucking right up against the snubbin' post. While he was sort of around on the other side I got the cinches drawed up tight. Then Wrangler chewed on his ear again while I untied the hackamore reins.

I gathered that heavy mane up in my left hand with the reins drawed tight. With my right hand I held the reins and the saddle horn at the same time. I held him this way so if he tried to pull away from me he wouldn't have a chance to kick me in the belly. He'd be forced around toward me, and about the worst he could do was step on me with both front feet.

"Turn 'im loose," I yelled. Wrangler did just that and let out a yell that sounded like a choked coyote. That old bay didn't know how to buck very hard but he was sure trying to learn. He crashed into the corral until I reached over and whopped him across the nose with a loaded quirt. It took several whops before he quit trying to tear my leg off against that pole corral. Now, I never was much of a quirt man, but there's times if you'll apply it good and hard right where the colt sucks you'll discourage a lot of bucking. This was one of those times. The bay soon settled down and either balked or sort of crow-hopped around, making a very feeble effort to buck.

Wrangler rode the brown with his spurs in his neck, yelling and kicking hell out of him every time he left the ground. The brown bucked out ahead and then turned back and went up again, coming down with all four legs stiff as a bunch of fence posts.

This kind of thing went on for three days except for some of the time we had been riding outside. Now, to make horse breaking easy you need two cowboys—one on the bronc and one on a gentle, well-broke horse. This way if the bronc tries to cut your leg off on a barbwire fence or jump off a bluff, your partner can ride in front of him or gather up your hackamore reins and wrap them around his saddle horn. That is the sensible way and the safest way to break horses. Do you think that's the way we did it for Jim Ed's outfit? Hell no! That was too slow. He wanted both his horse breakers riding in different directions at once, just bucking and raising hell. I think when he was off in town, checking in at the bank to count his money, that he could picture all this in his mind. I know damned well he kept himself laughing all the time just thinking about what was going on back at the ranch.

On the fourth morning I stood there with my rope in my hand and looked first at the roan, then at Wrangler. He looked just like a groundhog coming up for air when he crawled out of his bedroll in the morning, and he didn't look a hell of a lot better now except that I stood so far above him I couldn't see much but the brim of his hat and his potbelly hanging out over his droopy britches. What his britches was hanging on I don't know. They looked like they would drop right down around his knees any minute, but that was as far as they would have gone. His legs was bowed so bad that if you was to straighten them up he would be twice as tall.

"How old you think that roan is, Wrangler?"

"I reckon he's about seven or eight."

"Jim Ed says he's a fiver."

"If Jim Ed says he's a fiver, time has been passing a hell of a lot faster than Jim Ed thinks."

"I bet he's nine if he's a day," I said.

"Look at his teeth and see," said Wrangler kind of funny-like.

"Well, now," I said, "I figured I'd let you take him over, seein' as how that brown has been givin' you so much trouble. It'll give you a chance to rest up and get the soreness out of your bones."

"Naw, I reckon I'll just let you go ahead with him," says Wrangler real kind, like I was his baby sister. "Seein' as how Jim Ed wants a fancy pony made out of him and you're so much better at reinin' a horse out than me."

We stood there and jawed back and forth for a spell. I could see there wasn't a thing to do but take in after the roan. Maybe he wasn't spoiled. Maybe them marks in his shoulder was put there to stop some good honest bucking. Maybe he'd quit then and settled down to make a good, gentle cow horse. Maybe.

Well sir, I pitched out the catch rope, and the roan turned to me kinda quiet-like and looked right down that rope like he was staring down a gun barrel. He didn't wiggle a hair. I put the hackamore on him and tied him to the corral fence. Hell, I didn't need the snubbing post, as gentle as the old roan was. Besides, Wrangler had that bucking brown tied up to it.

Wrangler was acting kind of peculiar. He'd rear back on them squatly hocks of his and kick that brown in the belly just as hard as he could. The brown would hump up so the saddle looked like it had a big watermelon under it. Then Wrangler would look at the ground under his belly, step back, and kick again. When he stopped to look at the ground under the brown for about the fifteenth time, I just plain had to go see what the hell he was doing. I saw what he was after, all right. There was a wet foamy spot there in the corral dust. Wrangler seemed satisfied now and mounted the brown for about the twentieth time and started reining him around the corral. Seems like that kidney action kind of gentled the brown down some.

I rubbed my hand across the roan's shoulder, feeling all them spur scars. "You must of been a mean son of a bitch when you was a colt," I said. The roan looked like he had gone to sleep on me. I crawled under the hackamore reins kind of careless-like to get around on the other side and see how bad he was scarred up over there.

"*Ouch!*" Good Lord a'mighty, a bear must have reached through the corral poles and bit about half my back off! I whipped around hollering to beat hell. Right there in the same spot stood the old roan with a patch of my shirt hanging out of his jaws. I felt up my back where there was a big chunk of meat missing.

"Wrangler," I yelled, "this Goddam roan is a cannibal!"

Well now, about half mad and still hurting, I saddled that horse up. I jerked the cinch so tight it almost cut him in two. He didn't even grunt. I took my catch rope and flipped it around the saddle horn and threw my hat under him and hollered as loud as I could. He walked off like he was carrying the Queen of England to a church meeting.

Sometimes if you are in a hurry to get someplace and don't want to dirty up a new shirt or something, you can buck an old pony out with just the saddle on his back, then mount and ride off about your business. It didn't work this time.

I led him over in the corner of the corral so if he tried to pull away from me the posts would stop him. I eased up in the saddle and turned him out in the corral. Now I'm saying right now that this old roan had the best rein on him I ever saw. Just start to turn him and he was already around, swinging smooth and quick with his head down like a good cutting horse.

I told him, "Roan, I don't mind you bitin' hell out of me, but I wish you hadn't tore my shirt."

Just when I was beginning to feel proud of this good cutting horse he let a big windy and took a run straight at the corral. As easy-mouthed as he was a minute before, you would think I could have turned him back, but it didn't turn out that way. I was busting a gut trying to turn him, but he just gathered speed and jumped right up on top of the corral. Over he went, smacking the ground like a ton of dead beef and knocking the wind out of both of us. I fell free and jumped up before he did. I had a lot more air than I could handle. My lungs were bouncing around like a hog's belly.

When the old roan stumbled to his feet I was on him. He took off in a run again. His legs was still wobbly when he started bucking. Now I had the jump-go on this bag of bones. I had my right hand around that saddle horn like it was the doorknob to heaven's gate, and my right elbow was crimped down over my hipbone like a vise.

I was pulling up on them hackamore reins like I was dragging a pot of gold out of a deep well. But it just didn't do any good. That son of a bitch bogged his head and jumped way off out toward the Arizona border and came down hard on his front legs, driving them in the ground plumb to bedrock, the way it felt to me. The next jump was just as high and just as long, but when he drove into the ground again he was headed toward the Texas border, and in between that old roan horse was sure tearing hell out of the state of New Mexico.

I stayed till I lost my hat. I stayed till I lost a stirrup. I stayed till I lost both stirrups, and a while longer after that. It just didn't do any good. The world was jumping around and going in crazy circles, and eleven hundred pounds of horseflesh was pounding my behind to pieces. Then I flopped around in the pure, clean, fresh mountain air like a baby bird and came down on my back right where the roan had bit me. It was a very poor feeling.

I rolled over and looked around. The roan was in a dead run headed back for the corral. For a minute I thought he was going to jump back in, but he came to a sliding halt and looked back at me with his head up high.

I shook my fist at him and yelled kind of weak-like, "I'll make you as gentle as a milk-pen calf if I have to kill you doin' it."

I could see Wrangler off about a quarter of a mile trying to rein the brown back toward the corral. He was having his own troubles. I got up and hobbled along toward the roan. Wrangler beat me there. He set on the brown holding the roan's hackamore reins.

"Hell's fire, he sure fooled hell out of me," I said. "That's what I'll call him. Old Fooler."

"Bucks harder'n I figgered," said Wrangler, glancing sideways at Old Fooler.

"You never know what a dog's eaten till he shits," I said, grabbing the reins. I mounted that Fooler horse and dug the spurs in his shoulders—hard. He wouldn't buck a jump—just moved out, flinching a little now and then from the steel.

Wrangler tried to follow, but he made several figure eights and a backtrack on the way. Now things were looking up. Wrangler had got his horse to where he could turn him around inside a hundred acres, and Old Fooler was moving out in the prettiest running walk I ever seen. I had him reining again, and I began to perk up. Well, there is where I learned something basic about that horse. Not that it did me much good, but I had the pleasure of the knowledge just the same. When things looked best he was at his worst. He broke into a run, circling like we were on a racetrack. I reared back on the hackamore, jerking and cussing.

We came to a little gully about twenty feet deep and ten feet across. By God, I damn near died right then! It looked like he was going to jump right in it. He was running with his ears laid back and legs stretching for strange country. Hell's fire, he sailed up and out and across that gully like he was one of them fancy horses military men jump around at horse shows. He came down on the other side and wheeled, running parallel to the gully as fast as he could move his legs.

I could see old Wrangler up ahead and I yelled, "Rope the son of a bitch before he falls into the canyon!"

I didn't know if he heard or not. I kept imagining Old Fooler was running with both feet on the left side hitting nothing but clean, pure, fresh mountain air out over the gully and two feet on the right side lapping about halfway over the brim. I saw Wrangler throw a big loop at us, turn the brown, and spur him away from the gully.

When I could see again, I gazed upon a very strange sight. I could see the bellies of two horses. The roan was stretched out a few feet in front of me. A little farther on, the brown was lying in the same position. There was just one thing wrong. That brown had six legs and two of them was real short and had high-heel boots on the ends.

I stumbled up, limped over to the roan, and got him on his feet. Then the brown got up, shaking his head and looking over at the roan. He wasn't paying any attention to poor old Wrangler lay-ing there so peaceful and quiet. I looked down at Wrangler, expect-ing to have to say some prayers over him. He was turning blue, and I figgered that if he was dead he wouldn't have started turning so fast. So I got ahold of his arms and started pumping them up and down. Pretty soon he made a noise like a turkey gobbler makes that has the croup. I kept pumping. The noise got louder.

I said, "You all right, Wrangler?"

He finally said, "Yeah, but tell the bartender to quit servin' that cheap whiskey."

It was a day or two before Wrangler got his right mind back, what there was of it. But he got up and helped me untangle the rope from around the broncs. I got back on the roan and Wrangler got back on the brown. We didn't really want to, but it was a three-quarter-mile walk back to the corral. I sat kinda stiff-like with my hind end screwed right down into solid leather. Old Fooler moved out smooth and easy, just fox-trotting to beat sixty. Just as gentle as a milk-pen calf . . .

TWO

Three days later I crawled out of my bunk. I felt like I had been beat across the back by a ten-foot giant swinging a brand-new wagon tongue. Sore? I reckon I was.

If it hadn't been for the smell of Wrangler making coffee and cooking up some sowbelly and biscuits, I would have quit right there. I can't remember when a boot was so hard to pull on, considering how skinny I am. Seems like that boot had shrunk and my foot had swelled. Finally, though, I got upright. Then the hard part commenced. One hip was hanging about two inches lower than the other and my knee joints was just plain locked solid.

I was hoping Old Fooler was in the same condition.

"Wrangler," I said, "if that Old Fooler horse don't slack off before long, I am goin' to take a sharp ax and hit him right between the eyes."

"Ain't no use ruinin' a good ax," Wrangler said, reaching into the oven and pulling out a pan of brown hot biscuits.

"Maybe you're right," I said, pouring me some coffee in a big tin cup. I finally got settled down at the old splintery table and washed about a quart of coffee down my gullet. It limbered me up enough so I could slice off a chunk or two of sowbelly and eat about two thirds of them biscuits.

"Now ain't that just like that Goddam Jim Ed to take all the other hands over east for the fall roundup and leave me and you here by ourselves with that pen full of spoiled horses?"

"Just like him," said Wrangler. "Sometimes I wish I was back wranglin' dudes."

"How come you ever quit and took a job on a underpaying, overworked outfit like this?" I asked.

Now old Wrangler is usually making a long speech if he grunts twice, but once in a while he will bust loose and you can't hardly shut him up. He swallowed a biscuit whole and squinted out of a face that looked like a bulldog that had run headfirst into a big mule's hind foot and said, "A woman."

"A what?" I said.

"A woman by the name of Toy Smith," he said.

"Mighty pretty name," I said.

"Mighty pretty woman," he said.

"Well, God a'mighty, quit wastin' all this time and *tell* me about it!" I yelled.

"I was workin' for that Castle Rock outfit over near Phoenix," he said. "You heard of it, ain't you?"

"Yeah," I said, wanting to kick him in the belly for holding up the story.

"Well," he went on, "it's one of them fancy outfits caterin' to all them rich people from back East and out in California. They have these here hot springs all around the headquarters, and they got 'em rocked in like a regular windmill tank."

"You mean like a swimmin' pool?" I asked.

"You might say that," Wrangler agreed. "Anyway, there wasn't nobody there that wasn't rich or aimin' to be soon. I had this job of takin' these dudes out for a moonlight ride among the cactus and cookin' up a meal over the campfire. Then I'd play a git-tar and sing somethin' or other."

This last pretty near ruined my breakfast because I have never seen a cowboy that could play a guitar worth a damn, much less sing so you could stand to listen. Least of all Wrangler, who had a voice like a rusty hinge.

"What in the hell did you sing?" I asked.

"Oh, I don't know," said Wrangler, "I just run a bunch of words together and beat on them guitar strings. But that's what started all the trouble with Toy Smith," he went on. "Seems like she thought I was a great primitive singer."

"What's that?"

"How in the hell would I know?" said Wrangler. "Just the same, at nights when we got back and I got the horses unsaddled and fed, there would be Toy Smith hangin' over the corral gate waitin' for me to go for a swim in them hot-water tanks. She sure was a swimmer," said Wrangler. "And float! Hell, she looked like a whole mountain range lyin' out there on her back."

"Was she big?" I asked.

Wrangler looked at me and snorted through his flat nose. "Big? Why, Dusty, you couldn't get her in a hay barn without widenin' the doors."

I figured he was stretching it a little, but I got the drift that this Toy woman was on the generous side.

"She got to where she follered me every place I went except the toilet. Ever' time we'd have a dance for the cowboys and dudes, she just grabbed little old me and waltzed all night. I couldn't see past her for all that belly and there weren't no use lookin' up, for there was about forty pound of bosom hangin' over my head. There was just one thing to do and that was hold on tight and pray. She was all right as far as that part goes, but I began to get that crowded-in feelin'. You know, like you get in a cave with just one way out and a mama bear blockin' your trail. She kept tellin' me how much she loved me and that if I hitched up with her I'd never have to work another day in my life."

"You crazy damn fool," I said. "She was rich and you passed up your chance to tie on to her?"

"I didn't just exactly pass it up," said Wrangler, sort of sad-like. "It's just that things happened to alter the course of true love, as them dudes say. She got me to comin' over to her room ever' night after our swim."

"Naturally," I said.

"But seems," said Wrangler, "that she wasn't the only one that liked my cookin' and this er . . . uh . . . prim—primitive singin'. This other gal was about half as big and twice as purty. One night I told Toy to go on to bed—that I had to shoe a horse and would see her somewhat later."

"Whoever heard of shoein' a horse at night?" I said.

"Well, Toy Smith did," Wrangler said. "I went for a little ride and a little swim with this here other little tender thing. I never figgered that Toy would get up and check on me."

"You just can't tell about true love, can you?" I said.

"Naw, you sure cain't, Dusty," he said. "Anyway, 'long just before daybreak I come sneakin' into Toy's room as quiet as a country kid in a new suit of clothes. I eased down on the bed and pulled one boot off. Then I felt something hard and cold sticking out from under her piller."

"What was it?" I asked, my mind having jumping fits.

"It was a ball-peen hammer," Wrangler said, as if that was the end of the world. "I eased my boot back on, listenin' to Toy breathe heavy as a foundered mare. Then I sneaked out of there and headed for the barn. I got my horse and saddle and loaded them in the pickup, expectin' any minute to feel that ball-peen hammer drove plumb to the handle in my skull. When I started that pickup it sounded like seventeen water barrels rollin' off a steep mountain. I lit out for Phoenix and hunted me up a bar. Well, I found one where I had made some friends before, and stayed there watchin' the door for Toy Smith. About two or three days later one of the hired hands came in, knowin' where I might be. He said he had a message for me. I called him off in a far corner and a deep booth and ordered two double shots and said, 'Shoot.' He said to me, 'Wrangler, Toy is kinda mad. She said her branch of the Smith family didn't lie and they didn't steal and when she says she aimed to kill Wrangler Lewis, that is exactly what she meant.'

"Now," Wrangler went on, breathing kind of heavy, "knowin' how set in her ways Toy was and how honest this cowboy was, I decided it was time to move on."

"Well, that explains how come you went to work for a sorry outfit like this," I said.

"Yeah, sometimes I wish I'd of faced old Toy instead," he said. "By the way, how come you're workin' on this no-good ranch?"

"Now, Wrangler," I said, "you know damn well it's because I'm so dumb. Ain't it right plain that any cowboy who'd ride that Old Fooler horse more than once is just plumb ignorant?"

"Reckon you're right," he said.

I hated to face it, but knew I couldn't stall it off much longer. Old Fooler was out there in the horse pasture waiting for me to come and get him. I finished off what biscuits was left and rolled me a smoke. Wrangler poured us both another cup of coffee.

"Just think," I said, "of all the fun the rest of the boys are havin' down there gatherin' those cattle and cuttin' out the calves and all the ropin' and brandin' and no tellin' what else is goin' on. It makes me kinda sick to think about it. That cockeyed Jim Ed Love don't have no consideration for horse breakers a tall."

"Don't nobody else, neither," said Wrangler.

"Reckon you're right," I said. "If it's all the same with you, I'll go wrangle the horses while you clean up this mess."

"Whatever suits you just tickles me plumb to death," said Wrangler. Well, I saddled the night horse and loped out into the horse pasture.

It wasn't long till I had that Roman-nosed, walleyed, spur-marked bunch of critters back in the corral. That mean-ass, bald-face roan led them in. By the time I unsaddled the night horse I'd limbered up somewhat. Pretty soon Wrangler came out. We roped us a couple of mounts, snubbled them up, and turned the rest out.

Wrangler looked at me kinda queer. "You ain't goin' to take on that roan again today, are you?" he asked.

"Got to," I said. "He's gainin' on me now."

Well sir, it was a day to remember for a long time to come. Me and Wrangler rode out of there on what was beginning to look like a couple of old-time ranch horses. He had his little black working the reins good and was even getting him used to the bits. I was still using the hackamore on the roan, trying to get his nose as raw and sore as I could.

We strung out across the half-mile down to a section line fence. That roan rolled along so smooth a man was tempted to forget what he really was. I guess I did for a minute. I got down to open the gate, pulled it back, and let Wrangler ride through. Just as I stepped back to hook the wire loop over the gatepost, I felt something jerk at the reins, then something heavy hit me in the belly. The son of a bitch had pulled loose and kicked me all at the same time. I was bent over trying to get rid of excess wind.

"Wrangler," I croaked, "let me have your horse."

He stepped down and I crawled on. Old Fooler had run off a ways and then stopped to graze peaceably, as if nothing had happened at all.

"I'll be back in a minute," I yelled at Wrangler. Old Fooler had got himself in a jam this time. He'd gone too far. Here is where I would fix him once and for all. Off to the right a fifty-foot-wide arroyo cut in toward the fence, making a triangle. It had a ten- to twenty-foot drop-off, so I figured Old Fooler wouldn't try to jump it, and I didn't think he was crazy enough to jump *into* it. I spurred the black toward him, undoing the leather thong from around the catch rope, flipping the honda over the saddle horn, shaking out a loop and cussing Old Fooler all at once.

He threw his head up and took off for the far corner. The dust was boiling up and the triangle was getting more pointed all the time. I could feel the black stretching to beat hell under me, but I still spurred for more. Old Fooler was glancing over at the arroyo, wondering what he had overlooked, when I rode up on him.

I didn't get to use my rope this go-round. The first thing I knew I was riding stirrup leather against stirrup leather. The arroyo was crowding Fooler on one side, and the barbwire fence was scratching at me from the other. And it wasn't getting any wider. If I kept going I would lose a leg on the wire. If Fooler kept going he would fall off into the arroyo. I just couldn't make myself stop. Pretty soon that triangle came to a sharp point and there was just one place left to go. We all went down over the side, and I mean down. I don't know how it happened but I landed on my feet still holding the reins, right in the middle of a bunch of kicking horseflesh.

When the dust cleared, the black was struggling to his feet. He was real shook up. I could see Old Fooler's tracks in the soft bottom of the arroyo. The black got his wind back in a dead run because I climbed back aboard and spurred him down the arroyo, gathering up my rope at the same time.

It seemed like we ran down that hot, dusty, washed-out ditch for a long time. Finally, Old Fooler found a place to get out, and he did. I spurred the sweating black right up after his tracks. All I could see when we topped out was a long streak of dust heading for some low cedar-covered hills about a mile away. It's a fool thing to do to try to catch a loose horse out in the open from the back of another. There is just too much difference in what they're carrying. Besides, Old Fooler could run like a rabbit dog. But then, like I told Wrangler, I was stupid anyway, and on top of that I was mad.

We just kept going and when we finally hit timber I started tracking. Old Fooler, not knowing this part of the country, was headed into a barbwire corner. This corner set out in an opening, and if I could get my rope on him I would drag him to death.

Sure enough, there he was. He charged down the fence to the right and I cut across, swinging a big loop. The black was so tired I could feel him wobbling under me. It looked like Old Fooler was going to get away this time, too. He was a long way out.

I threw the loop anyway. It seemed like the slowest loop in the world. It just floated and shrunk the farther it went, and then Old Fooler ran his head into what was left of it. The black had already set up, not from experience but from being so tired. This gave us the advantage.

Old Fooler went up and over and around and down. Just as he scrambled to his feet, I spurred hard sideways and jerked both of us down. Well, it wasn't much of a fall because there wasn't much speed left in any of us. When me and the black got up, Old Fooler did the same. He was about half choked, but he trotted right over to us just like he was going to apologize and love us to death. Of course, the old devil simply wanted to loosen the rope from around his neck. Just like a house dog, he followed me back to Wrangler.

Wrangler was lying in the shade of a post, asleep. He sat up, pulling his hat back down on his head. "I thought you said you was just goin' to be gone a minute," he said.

"Time flies," I said.

I took the rope from around Old Fooler's neck and handed

Wrangler the reins of the black. Then I walked up and yelled just as loud as I could and kicked Old Fooler in the belly. He jumped straight up with all four feet and I set back with all I had on those hackamore reins. You talk about hitting the ground—well, that old pony jarred the world right down to the deep-water level. He got up. I hollered and kicked him again. He just stood there this time, humping up a little. I kicked till I couldn't lift my sore leg anymore. I hollered till nothing but a sick whisper came out of my throat. He wouldn't budge.

I got my breath and said to Wrangler, "Now what you goin' to do about a horse like that?"

He didn't have an answer. I didn't have one either.

I was beginning to wonder if Old Fooler was going to break me before I did him. In fact, I felt right then that one of us would just plain have to kill the other.

THREE

The boys came back from the fall roundup. They had delivered the stock to town, loaded it into cattle cars, and Jim Ed had gone to Denver to see to the final delivery. In a few days he would be back with another bankful of money to his credit. The boys kept going on about what a time they'd had in town, telling one big lie after another.

I got so disgusted about missing out on all this that I just went out to the corral, saddled Old Fooler, and rode off by myself. Now wasn't that a dumb thing to do?

This horse had me slightly boogered. You would figure that most horses would come nearer bucking downhill than up. You would be right, except for Old Fooler. I don't say he bucked uphill exactly. It amounted to the same thing, though. I learned this a very hard way.

I was watching him real close as I rode across the ripened grama-grass-covered hills. We moved down into this little draw and started up the other side. Just as we topped out, he fired. Naturally, the saddle slips back a little when a horse is pulling upgrade, but the way Old Fooler jumped it had lapped right over his rear end. He lunged way out and kicked back with both hind feet. It snapped my head back like the tip end of a bullwhip. My teeth chipped enamel at every jump.

Well, I made one mistake I would never make again with Fooler. If you can use a loaded quirt, that's fine. It will take a lot of sass out of some pretty mean horses. I raised it up high and took a hard swing, aiming to hit Old Fooler right between the ears. I didn't much care if he did fall on me. I figured this might help us both. I should have kept my right hand on that saddle horn where it belonged, though, for all I hit was air. I smacked the ground like a dead buzzard.

It was about three miles by bird travel to the gate opening into home pasture. That was where Old Fooler was headed. He was still bucking, and I could see them stirrups clanging together above his back. Then he disappeared over a rise and there wasn't a thing to keep me company but one little white cloud about a thousand miles off over the northern mountains. I saw that cloud when I looked up at the sky and asked the Lord to please not let me kill myself and to give me the wings of an angel so I could fly after that horse and break his Goddam neck.

Well, the Lord answered the first part of my prayer, for in about an hour and a half I'd forgot all about killing myself. I was hurting so bad I figured I would die anyway. I walked and walked, and a big blister grew on one foot. I pulled off my boot to ease the pain. When I tried to put it back on she just wouldn't go. That foot had swelled up bigger than the hole in the top of that boot. I started to take my pocket knife and make that hole bigger. Then I thought this over and decided against it. My foot would mend—the boot wouldn't.

I walked and I walked. I cussed and I cussed. I hoped that black-hearted Fooler horse heard some of the things I called him. He would be ashamed of himself or awful proud, one. A hole wore in my sock. The sweat ran from under my hat and down into my eyes, and the bottom of my foot proved to be softer than the ground I walked on.

Pretty soon I limped about a yard deep on the barefoot side. The boot I was packing got heavier and heavier no matter which hand I carried it in. The sock wore plumb off the foot. There was a little bit of it hanging around my ankle to remind me what color it had been. If I just hadn't reached for that quirt I might have been sitting a horse, ready to get down and open the gate into headquarters right now.

I got back just before sundown. There stood Old Fooler at the gate, looking back at me with his head up high as if he was sure enough glad to see me.

I felt kind of embarrassed riding into camp with one boot off. The boys all laughed and wanted to know if I'd felt sorry about my horse carrying such a big load. They acted like I had just got down and walked on purpose. It would have been easy to have killed the whole bunch, including Old Fooler, right on the spot. I was just too tired to do it.

It took two days of soaking that foot in hot water before I could get the boot back on. On the third day I was back with Wrangler working the horses. But I can tell you for sure I was going to lay off that Fooler horse the first day.

We had topped out the whole bunch by now. Most of them were reining good and beginning to stop with their hind feet tucked up under their bellies like good horses should. They didn't buck more than once or twice a day now, and then not very hard. I had one big bay that I could tell was going to make a real working cow horse.

Just when everything was going our way and it looked like we might make a few head of good horses, Jim Ed showed up. He had plans. These plans concerned me and Wrangler. Now me and old Wrangler hadn't been to town since the Fourth of July, and we were beginning to get mighty thirsty for some of that high-powered town water with maybe two or three high-stepping females thrown in. Do you think that's what Jim Ed had in mind? Hell, no!

Jim Ed says in that purry voice of his, "Now, boys, I'm goin' to give you the chance of a lifetime. Down at the lower camp there is around a hundred and fifty, maybe a hundred seventy-five, strays that's gone wild on us. I want you boys to go down there and spend the winter gatherin' this stuff. It's a lot lower in elevation there. The snow don't hardly stay on the ground a tall. Why, it'll be a regular vacation for you."

I was just itching to tell Jim Ed where to go and how long he could stay for his vacation when he put the clincher on the argument.

"Boys," he said, rearing back and grinning so all the gold in his mouth glittered, "there is five dollars a head bonus for every head you gather. Cows, calves, steers, it don't make no difference. Five dollars a head! Did you ever hear anything like it?"

Just as he said this he threw a whole stack of five-dollar bills on the floor in front of where me and Wrangler stood staring bug-eyed. It worked.

We said, "Yeah, that sounds all right." I never knew of a couple of dumber cowboys than us.

We got in a couple of pack mules and slung the pack with sow-belly, dried peaches, beans, flour, the works. We got in the string of broncs, too.

Jim Ed said, "Boys, this will give you a chance to work your horses like they need to be worked. Sore backs and tender hoofs is what makes gentle horses." Then he walked over and picked up a whole armload of brand-new catch ropes. For a minute I was fooled into thinking Jim Ed was being considerate, but a little later, down at the lower camp, I realized different. We would need every one of those ropes before we got those wild cattle out of that wild country.

Well, we strung out with me riding lead on Old Fooler. I led the pack mules till they got used to following. Wrangler rode behind on the drag with the string of half-broke broncs in between.

If we kept going steady and didn't stop to admire the scenery, we could make it to Vince Moore's outfit for supper. I sure was anxious to see old Vince. It had been a long time. He was a good feller to my notion. Besides, he made the best bootleg whiskey in New Mexico.

Old Fooler didn't act up at all that day. He even moved out like he knew where we were going. I watched him careful and close, figuring he was just shoring up his energy.

The sun was still warm at midday, even though it was November. Along about the shank of the afternoon she began to cool down, but we rode hard, keeping a little sweat breaking out on the flanks of our mounts. Just before sundown I spotted Vince Moore's windmill. Then we saw his old wooden, unpainted, run-

down shack. It looked like the one we would be living in down at lower camp.

When we got about a hundred yards of the house, the dogs started barking—hound dogs, collie dogs, and just dogs. I bet there wasn't a rabbit in five miles of Vince's outfit. Damn if he wasn't up on the crow's nest working on his windmill. He yelled down, "Well, I'll be. Where in the hell did you boys come from?"

I said, "Vince, I hope we are just in time for supper."

"The woman'll have it ready in about half an hour," he said. "Say, why don't one of you boys get down and help me with this here windmill. It'll only take a minute."

Now, if there is one thing I hate worse than a diamondback rattler, it's a windmill. That is the only thing I could figure in Jim Ed's favor: his whole ranch was watered by springs—not a windmill on the whole place except at headquarters.

I yelled back, "Vince, you get down and ride out two or three of these old ponies, and I will climb up there and fix your windmill."

Vince didn't say anything more about the windmill. "Go ahead and turn your horses loose in the corral, boys. Pitch 'em some hay out of the stack and I'll be done here directly."

This we proceeded to do.

Then Vince yelled, "Go on over to the house, boys, and wash up. Don't use too much water, though. Been kinda short ever since this windmill's been givin' trouble." Well, he had been kind of short of water for at least thirty years.

We walked over toward the house. Marthy, as Vince called her, met us on the porch. Four or five little kids and big kids were peeking around her. She was sort of sagging all over like a swaybacked mule. Her dress wasn't quite clean. Her hair hung straight down in little wads like a horse's mane that's full of cockleburs. But she was glad to see us and that made her beautiful like she'd been before the hard times had worn her down.

"Why, howdy, boys. Haven't seen you in a long time. Where you headed?"

I said, "We're goin' to winter down in the lower-camp country, Marthy, and try to pick up a few strays for Jim Ed."

"Yeah, he's starvin' to death," said Wrangler.

"Like a fat hog," said Marthy. "Come on in and wash up, boys. You young-uns get out of the way now and let the gentlemen clean up."

"God a'mighty, Marthy, that ain't little Bobby, is it?" I asked.

"Yeah, that's him."

"He's growed a foot since I saw him summer a year ago. And look at Christine and Sally. Why, they're pretty near grown-up young ladies."

The kids just stood and twisted around and grinned, not saying a word. Vince believed in doing most of the talking in his family.

I know one thing, the Moores might not eat very fancy but they eat a whole lot. Marthy put the biggest pot of beans I ever saw on the table and about four pans of corn bread and some home-made butter. A gallon bucket full of coffee steamed on the stove. It got kind of hungry-like thereabouts.

Vince came in talking to beat hell, washed up, and everybody sat down at the splintery old homemade table and started lapping it up. Vince could eat faster than any of us and still keep on talking at the same time.

"How's Jim Ed?" he asked.

"Fine, I reckon," I said.

"How much did his calves weigh out this year?"

"They did right well, Vince," I said. "Weighed out right at four hundred pounds average."

"Man, that's good," Vince said. "I didn't have any to ship this year. Business ain't been too good."

I knew he was talking about his whiskey business because this little old one-man starvation outfit of his wouldn't make anybody a living. I knew too that before Jim Ed bought up just about every little outfit around, Vince had had a lot more customers.

We ate and talked and pretty soon we got down to the smoking and coffee-drinking stage. Vince was bragging on one of his hounds and telling how that hound could run right up beside a coyote and latch on to its throat and kill him all by himself. I knew this was mostly a big yarn, but I enjoyed it.

Pretty soon Marthy and the kids went to bed, and Vince said, "Would you boys care for a little snort?"

"Don't mind if I do," I said.

Wrangler said, "Whatever suits you just tickles me plumb to death."

Vince got up and went outside and came back in with a gallon jug. He got some tin cups and poured us all a big slosh.

"Well now, I reckon some fellers know how to make store-bought clothes, and some fellers can patch up an old wreck of a pickup so it runs like new, and some fellers can make lots of money like Jim Ed, but there ain't nobody makes better whiskey than you, Vince Moore," I told him.

That stuff rolled down my gullet just as smooth and warm as milk to a titty baby. Old Wrangler just kinda closed his eyes and leaned back against the wall, and that busted nose of his was flared out like a wolf in a henhouse. It was sure enough good.

"More?" Vince asked.

"Believe I will at that," I said.

"Yeah," said Wrangler.

Well sir, it was a fine evening, and after about four or five more cups of Vince Moore's special it got finer.

I asked Vince, "Did you see that good-looking blaze-faced roan I was a-ridin'?"

"First thing I noticed," said Vince.

"Did you ever see a runnin' walk like that?"

"Did seem like he moved easy and sure," said Vince.

"Listen, Vince," I said, kind of warming to my pitch, "that horse has got the best rein of any animal I ever rode. Ain't that right, Wrangler?" I said.

"He's got that if nothing else," said Wrangler.

"Nothing else?" I said, half sore-like. "Listen, he can run faster than a slim jackrabbit and stop before you even get the reins pulled back half tight. Vince, how about some more of that wonderful juice?"

"Sure, boys, just say when."

Vince filled them cups right up to the brim. I had to go into action quick to keep any of that precious liquid from spilling over and going to waste.

"Now, that Old Fooler horse was just made for a nice little outfit like yours, Vince," I went on. "You can work cattle on him, for one thing. And just to ride him is a pure pleasure, what with that runnin' walk you yourself noticed."

Vince was staring kind of red-eyed, and every once in a while he wiped the long gray hair back from where it was falling down over his ears.

"Now, Vince," I said, "you know how it is when one of them old hound dogs of yours, especially the one that can kill by hisself, gets in hot and heavy after a coyote."

"Yeah," Vince said, wiping his mouth with a creased, rough hand. "Yeah, I know."

"Well," I said, "you want to get in on the kill worse than anything else in the world. Ain't that right?"

"Yeah," he said, scratching his chin and blinking them little pig eyes that was something like Wrangler's, only redder.

"You haven't got any more worries about being there when you ride Old Fooler."

"He ain't my horse," said Vince.

"Now that's where you're dead wrong," I said. "For just a small consideration and just to show you how much we appreciate your hospitality to us here tonight, I'm goin' to let you have him."

"I ain't got a dime to my name," said Vince, moving that big rusty hand back up to his hair. "Not a penny."

"Good Lord, Vince, you didn't think I was wantin' money, did you? Here, hit me another slug of that wonderful stuff. All I want would be eight jugs of this stuff. It's gonna be a long winter down at the lower camp."

"Yeah, and dry," Wrangler said.

"Jim Ed said it was dry as a snuffbox down there. The snow don't stay on the ground a tall," I raved. I could see them little red eyes just strainin' with the effort to think.

"Well, I don't know, boys," he said.

I had one of them sinking feelings like I had been fell on by a thousand-pound bronc. I knew if I waited till morning, and Vince sobered up, he would never agree to the swap. I was a desperate cowboy. Just then nature lent me a kind, helping hand. About a mile to the north a coyote let out a howl, and all the dogs jumped up and went to barking and raising hell. I saw quick-like that Vince's blood was really pumping and singing him a song. Yes sir. The old coyote fever was on him.

That's when I put the clincher to him. "Vince, you can catch that yappin' son of a gun an hour after sunrise tomorrow and be right there when the old red dog puts the big bite on him." For a minute the red eyes went blank. Then they shone out real bright.

"It's a deal!" he said. Then he shook our hands and poured some more of that wonderful stuff all round.

After a while Vince said it was time to turn in, and slumped forward with his head on the table and went to sleep, the proud owner of one hell of a piece of horseflesh. Me and Wrangler stumbled out to our bedrolls and said good night to the stars.

It was a good breakfast Marthy served up about daylight the next morning, but she had a tough time getting anybody but the kids to eat. Finally, after a lake of coffee, we got the packs back on the mules. On each pack hung four jugs—two on each side. I was anxious to get the hell out of there before Vince decided to try Old Fooler out.

"It shore has been enjoyable," Wrangler said, trying to sound fancy.

"Mighty hospitable of you folks," I said, trying to sound even fancier. I reined the bay out front and we got out of there. I will admit that Old Fooler looked a little lonesome standing there with his head up over the top of the corral watching us ride off. I didn't tell him good-bye. My stomach felt like I had swallowed a bunch of snapping turtles mixed with rusty barbwire. Wrangler must have felt the same, because after a while he called for me to stop. He said he had something he wanted to tell me.

I stopped and said, "What is it you want to tell me?"

"I'm thirsty," he said.

I agreed that this was a very important announcement. We both got down and had a drink.

Wrangler said, "What you goin' to tell Jim Ed about Old Fooler?"

"I don't know yet," I said, "but if I ever see that mean son of a bitch again I am goin' to kill him and tell God he committed suicide."

We rode on down toward the lower camp but we didn't make very good time. Seems like we had made the mistake of taking our first drink out of the same jug. It seemed unfair to make a mule carry a lopsided load, so we had to stop every now and then to make sure things was kept evened up.

FOUR

There it was—Jim Ed's lower camp. Someone had homesteaded it long ago, but now it was lonesome as hell. The corrals and the dirty wooden shack needed fixing. It's a hell of a big country out there. You could look for a hundred miles in almost any direction except west. There the view was blocked by a long, rocky, piñon-covered mesa. I knew it was there we would find the wild cattle. Gathering them would be something else. There were hundreds of brush-covered canyons for them to hide in, and the rough country was going to be hard on men and horses.

We moved on down, turned the horses out to pasture, keeping one up for a night horse. We unpacked the mules and started straightening up the shack. It was in a hell of a mess. Two windows were out and dust was thick over everything. The last boys there had left dirty dishes all piled about. The rats had built nests all over the three rooms and the birds had roosted in the broken windows. The rotten shingles on the roof had blown away, leaving several holes you could have thrown a tomcat through.

I got tired of messing around the house. So I packed in about a dozen buckets of water and told Wrangler, "I reckon I better go get you some firewood and cut it up since you are goin' to do the cooking around here."

Wrangler just grunted and I sneaked out to saddle the night horse. I rode out a ways and threw a loop over a fairly good-sized dead piñon tree. Then I spurred the other way. It was about all the little sorrel bronc could do to drag it in.

I turned him loose in the corral again and collected the ax we had packed.

I don't like chopping wood worth a damn, but it's better than keeping house.

I lit into that tree, and about three hours later, just before sundown, I had enough wood to do Wrangler for a week or two.

I was sure surprised when I got back up to the house. Wrangler had everything in place and about half clean. Water was boiling on the old four-hole iron range and the coffee was hot. He had a pot of beans on that would simmer for several days and was frying hell out of a bunch of sowbelly. Besides that, he had started some sourdough bread. He looked comical as could be standing there with that flour sack tied around his middle. The sack dragged on the floor and you couldn't tell whether he was walking or rolling.

I said, "Wrangler, you're goin' to make somebody a hell of a fine wife one of these days."

"I hope she's rich instead of so damn good-lookin'," he said, dishing up the grub.

It was a fine supper, considering the condition of everything when we got there. We crawled in our bedrolls that night feeling almost at home.

The next day we were anxious to get back up in the hills and start locating the cattle. That bonus on each head didn't have anything to do with it, of course—we are just naturally industrious cowboys. However, we decided we'd better work around the place for a few days first. The holding pasture was in bad shape. It wouldn't do us any good to gather the stock if we couldn't hold it. We took a heavy set of wire pliers, wire stretchers, and staples and went to work. Every so often we would stop and pull four wires tight as a slopped hog's gut. Then we would clamp her down solid with staples. We patched up the water gaps by tying heavy rocks to the wire so the spring rains wouldn't wash them out so easy. We put up a wing about a hundred yards out at an angle from the gate. We set the posts deep and stretched the wire tight. We would have to pen the wild stock here, and this wing would help get them through the gate.

We checked the snubbin' post in the corral. It was cedar and still stout as a yearling bull. We reworked the corral by adding new poles here and there. It would do now to work the broncs in. Then we took a couple of rusty shovels, that didn't fit our hands at all, and cleaned out the spring in the gathering pasture. It had filled up with black mud. After a couple of days of this degrading labor the water ran fresh and clear.

I said, "Well, Wrangler, I reckon we're set for the winter. I don't know but what that Jim Ed didn't pull a fast one on us. Do you realize we'll just barely get out of here in time to make the Fourth of July rodeo in Hi Lo?"

"I'd given that a little thought," said Wrangler. "It will be exactly a year since we went to town last."

I thought on this a spell and it made me feel kind of cut off from the rest of the world. I tried to cheer us up by saying, "Yeah, but think of all the back wages we'll collect and that big bonus from gatherin' this wild stock. Why, Wrangler, we'll pitch one that will make history even in a wild town like Hi Lo." But it just didn't do any good.

We saddled up a couple of the rawest of the broncs and rode toward the mesa. We didn't aim to try any gathering for a couple of days. Our idea was to scout out where the main bunches were running. Then we would move in and get after them.

It was one of those days that makes a feller feel good whether he wants to or not. The birds were singing to beat sixty and the wind had died down so you could feel the warm fall sun. The grama grass was up almost stirrup high, and I was thanking my lucky stars that I didn't have to be worrying about Old Fooler. Then I wished I hadn't thought about that son of a bitch. It gave me a uneasy feeling right where I buckle my belt.

Well, in one sandy wash we found traces of fifteen or twenty head. We didn't see them, but we could tell by the droppings and the way the grass was tromped down that they were ranging in there. We rode damn near to the top, finding tracks crossing tracks of steers, bulls, and old mother cows with calves. About the fourth day we figured we had done enough tracking.

"Wrangler," I said, "how many head you gonna guess is here?"

"Over two hundred," he said.

"Well, Jim Ed guessed a hundred and twenty-five to a hundred seventy-five. Maybe they ain't all his."

"He wouldn't care. Look what he did to Vince Moore. Bought out all his customers. Why, it's got to where a honest bootlegger like old Vince cain't hardly make a living anymore."

"I sure know it," I said. "The country is goin' to hell in a hurry. If these ranchers keep buying these pickup trucks, there ain't goin' to be no use for horse breakers like us."

We had been reining the broncs over rocky ridges until my hands were sore and set like an eagle's claws, but every time one of them swallowed his head to buck I went down after those hackamore reins like they were made of velvet.

Like I said, I was sure enough glad I didn't have to ride Old Fooler with these sore hands, and was about to say so to Wrangler when damned if Vince Moore didn't come riding up on a little brown horse leading the bastard.

I swallowed my tongue and felt like all my blood had run right out through the soles of my boots. He was right up in front of the shack before I could speak.

"Why, hello, Vince. Sure nice to see you again so soon. Get down and tie your horses. Wrangler's putting a bunch of sourdough in the oven. How's the wife and kids? I reckon you got the windmill fixed. How's business? Gettin' any new customers for that wonderful product of yours? How's Marthy and the kids? Looks like it's goin' to be a long, dry winter, don't it? Seen Jim Ed lately? How's your hounds gettin' along? 'Specially that one that kills a coyote by hisself. How's Marthy and the kids?"

"Howdy," said Vince, sort of sour. He got down off his horse. Then he took Old Fooler out and turned him loose in the corral with the night horse. I stood there with my mouth still moving but nothing coming out.

Vince walked back up and says, looking me straight in the eye, "There's your goddam outlawed horse. I want my whiskey back. That is, if there's any left."

I said, "Whatever do you mean, Vince? You must be kiddin' old Dusty Jones."

"I am like hell," he says.

"What happened?" I asked, wishing I could go deaf before he answered.

"Well, in the first place, I went coyote huntin' on him the mornin' after you left. The first thing that happened, we jumped a big coyote not a half mile from the house."

"That's good," I said.

"No, that ain't good," Vince says. "I lined out on him like you told me, right behind the hounds."

"That's good," I said.

"That ain't good a tall," Vince said. "That son of a bitch can run, all right. He ran right on past where the dogs had that coyote down and he kept runnin' for about three miles. I didn't even have time to glance at the fight. We went by so fast I couldn't have seen nothin' but a blur anyway. When I finally got him turned around and headed back, the dogs had tore that coyote into so many pieces he looked like a fresh cow turd in a cyclone."

I opened my mouth but decided I might catch cold or something, so I shut it and listened to Vince rave on.

"The next mornin' I saddled him up in the corral and walked around pretty as you please, and just when I was feelin' like the day before had been a accident, it happened."

Wrangler rolled up to the door in his flour-sack apron and was fool enough to ask, "What happened?"

Vince did not need any urging. He said, "He bucked off about a mile and stopped and went to eatin' my good grass."

"A spirited horse like him gets hungry," I said.

Vince didn't pay any attention to this. He had other things on his mind. "Well, that made me so damn mad I figgered if I couldn't ride the ornery bastard, maybe I could plow with him. I been wantin' to put in some winter wheat anyway."

"How did he work?" that foolish Wrangler asked.

"Work!" Vince screamed. "He ran off with the plow and got it hung in a fence and tore down at least two hundred yards of good stout posts and barbwire and then he broke up all my harness. I've been several days and nights tryin' to get the whole damn place stuck back together." He stopped and choked a minute, then said, "I want my whiskey back."

There wasn't a thing to do but give it back. Howsomever, I talked him into leaving one jug for medicine, seeing as how we were so far from a doctor. He went on cussing Old Fooler until I was downright embarrassed.

So I made the mistake of saying, "Vince, I'm sure sorry this turned out like it did. But I think it was just one of those things, you know. Some people, good people, too, just can't get along with each other. I think that's the way it is with you and Old Fooler. Why, he never gives me a bit of trouble."

"That so?" says Vince. "Let's see you saddle him up and kick him into a dead run, then."

Well, I felt just like a dog caught sucking eggs. I was trapped. I moseyed out to the corral trying to act like my guts wasn't tying themselves in big sheepshank knots, and threw the rigging on Old Fooler. I said to him, "Now, you old bastard, just this once, please don't buck. Please."

Old Fooler stood there half asleep, his eyelids drooped down. He didn't even bother to switch his tail at a horsefly that was trying to swallow him whole. In fact, he was leaning so heavy on one side it looked like he might just fall over. I untracked him and stepped aboard. He walked around the corral easy and slow. I could feel the sweat running down my back.

"Well," says Vince, "you ready for me to turn him out?"

"Yeah," I croaked, just above a whisper. What I had in mind was to ease him out when Vince opened the gate, then get him into a lope and make for the nearest timber, where I could hide out, as quick as I could. It didn't work out. Vince had barely got the gate undone when Old Fooler went rocketing out through it.

He was bucking like mad but running at the same time. Vince was knocked six ways from Sunday and I was milking hell out of that saddle horn. Away we went. I could see he was headed for another arroyo. That goddam horse must have had one of them arroyos for a mother, the way he liked to fall in their laps. I decided to change the act and started digging my left spur up in his shoulder and bending them hackamore reins to the right. It worked. Slow but sure.

There was a deep bog off a ways to the right. If there's anything that will slow down a bucking horse and take the flint out of him, it's a deep bog. Old Fooler jumped smack dab in the middle of it and came to a sudden stop. *Boy*, I thought, *I've got you at last!* I knocked about two pounds of hair out of his shoulders and sides. He didn't even twitch. I reckon I could have killed him and he would have fell over dead before he would buck. Old Fooler had been there before.

I spurred and spurred. The horse hair was in my eyes and my mouth, and my legs were getting heavy and numb. It just didn't do any good. Finally I quit spurring, and cussed till I couldn't think of anything else to call him. This took quite a bit of time. Then I gently reined him out of the bog like I was helping my crippled grandmother to a rocking chair and rode back toward the house. I turned him out in the pasture. He threw up his tail and ran off looking for the other horses just like he owned the outfit.

"I'll get you yet if I have to run you off a thousand-foot bluff onto a bunch of sharp rocks," I yelled, waving my fist at his rump. I walked back to the house. "Where's Vince?" I asked Wrangler.

"He got his wonderful stuff and left while you was out in the bog."

"I hope he wasn't mad," I said.

"Naw," said Wrangler. "He just said he hoped Old Fooler kicked your eyeballs right out between your ears."

"Oh," I said.

FIVE

Everything was ready. The serious work started. Me and Wrangler was mighty earnest about that five-dollar-a-head bonus. It could be one hell of a big Fourth of July if we even made a 50 percent gather.

First we jumped three mother cows and a four-year-old steer. They tore through the brush like a dose of salts. The broncs plowed right in after them, with me and Wrangler setting aboard ducking limbs, reining around boulders, feeling the brush pull and drag at us like the devil's own claws. That's why cowboys wear heavy leather chaps. Without them, there wouldn't have been enough meat left on our leg bones inside of ten minutes to feed a dying sparrow hawk.

When we couldn't see stock we could hear them. For a while it didn't look like we were going to get anywhere. The big steer cut back and I cut back with him. The brush was so thick and the rocks so big that I either had to let him go or risk losing the cows and calves. I turned back and went in after Wrangler. We had them headed downhill in a dead run. If we could keep them that way till we hit the flats we had a good chance. We made it.

One old cow turned back again and again. The half-bronc sorrel I was riding didn't know what to do. I just had to whip him in the

37

side of the head with my hat and spur hell out of him, all the time working them hackamore reins like they were a steering wheel to head that ornery cow.

Finally I got mad, and when she turned back for the tenth time I spurred up and dropped a loop around both horns. I kept spurring one way and she headed the other. It was quite a shock to her when all the slack pulled out of the rope. She came back and over and my little old bronc damn near went down. I threw my weight over on one side, ramming the spurs to him at the same time. He stayed up and held, turning to face down the rope like I'd been training him to do. It was all over quick-like. I had the rope off the cow's horns and was back on my horse before she got her wind back. From then on she headed the way I wanted her to.

There was no slowing up now. We came downhill in a long hard lope. Three cows, three calves—thirty dollars on the hoof. That's a lot of money—to a working cowboy.

They hit that wing we had built and whirled around looking for an opening, but we crowded in just right and got them through the gate. I got down and slammed it shut, grinning all over. While the sweat dried on our horses, me and Wrangler had us a smoke and got a little clean, fresh pure mountain air into our lungs.

I said, "God a'mighty, thirty dollars in one day. This ain't never happened to me before."

Wrangler said, "Me neither."

I said, "I wish the Fourth of July was just next month."

Right then we figured we would have been the two richest cowboys ever to make a country rodeo. However, there was a whole long cold winter between us and the Fourth of July.

We went four more days before we penned another head. But little by little, one, two, three at a time, we gathered the stock out of the brush. We were sure enough doing what Jim Ed wanted. We were gathering his stock and putting sore backs and tender feet on the broncs at the same time.

The mother cows came first. They were easier to gather than the wild fat dry cows and the big, longer-legged steers. When we got to these last, things would really get wild on the mesa.

Finally, though, we had quite a bunch. We decided to pen what we had and hold a branding. These calves weighed in at between four and five hundred pounds and were as fat and slick as wagon grease on a peeled limb.

We penned them at the corral. Then we cut the mother cows out and checked the branding irons in the fire.

Wrangler said, "Just a little while more and they'll be ready."

I got the blackleg vaccine in the needle and sharpened my knife, getting ready to make a lot of little steers out of a lot of little bulls. Ever since I can remember I've liked a branding.

I remember when I was back home with Pa on his little leased outfit. We used to invite all the neighbors over for the brandings. The women brought something cooked, like chicken, hogside, pies, and cakes. We made a real to-do out of it. There was plenty of hands to help. The women and little bitty kids watched from on the corral fence while the bigger kids like me and the old hands went to work.

There were two fires and always one old boy who was good at heelin' calves. He took great pride in this. A calf is lots easier to handle with the rope around his heels instead of his neck. Two of us would go down the rope just as the roper dragged the calf close to the fire. We jerked in opposite directions, one on the rope, the other on his tail. Down he would go. While one man jumped on his heels, the other gathered up a foreleg with his knee in the calf's neck. We would hardly get him down before a cowboy was there burning a brand on him and another was cutting his testicles out if he was a bull, and at the same time he would earmark him and reach for the needle to shoot the blackleg vaccine to him.

The same thing would be going on at the other fire. We would brand a whole herd of calves in one day and have a big time doing it. After a while everybody would eat and drink some water or something. You just couldn't beat it.

Me and Wrangler were going about it a little bit different. These were big calves—wild and mean. We were shorthanded and had only a bunch of raw broncs and an outlawed roan son of a bitch to rope off of.

Wrangler said the irons was ready. He went out and fit a loop on a big whiteface calf. Then he fought his bronc around and started dragging him to the fire. I went down that rope and reached over his back with one hand in his flank and the other on the rope. The calf jumped straight up and kicked me in the belly with both feet. While he was up I heaved and down he went.

Wrangler bailed off his horse and came to help. In the meantime the calf had got one foot in my boot top and tore the bark off my shin. Then he kicked me in the mouth with the other foot. I had only one tooth in front that hadn't been broke, and now I didn't have that.

Wrangler pulled the calf's tail up between its kicking hind legs and held on while I tied all four feet with a four-foot piggin' string. Now, in rodeo they just tie three feet, but out here where we were you tied all four.

Wrangler went after the branding iron and started burning Jim Ed's JL brand on the calf's hip. I reached down and pulled the testicles as far out toward the front of the bag as I could. Then I split the bag and cut out the balls. I cut the fat off because that can cause infection, and swabbed the bag with pine tar. Then I cut a big chunk out of his ear called an earmark, which is part of a brand on every ranch. I cut off the little nubbin' horns and swabbed a little more pine tar on the holes. I shoved the needle in the loose folds of skin at his neck and pushed the plunger. The hair was burning and getting in my eyes and up my nose, but I could see that red-colored brand would stay there as long as that calf hide was in this world.

Wrangler went back and got on his horse and rode him up to give me slack in the rope. I took the loop off his head, undid the piggin' string, and turned this young ex-bull loose into the world, all fixed up so the blackleg wouldn't kill him and branded so some cattle thief couldn't make off with him. He now belonged to Jim Ed Love for sure.

Well, we handled about three more like this and I had all the wind kicked out of me and half my hide was peeled loose here and there. My mouth was swelled up and I was already missing that broken tooth.

I said to Wrangler, "I wish we had a good heelin' horse. We could sure save lots of work and wear and tear."

I decided I would try Old Fooler. It was a crazy notion, but strangely enough it worked. I never rode a better heelin' horse in my life. Old Fooler had been to lots of brandings. Wrangler would throw his loop around a calf's neck and start toward the fire with him. Then I'd ease Old Fooler in close, riding in the other direction. At just the right spot I would let my loop drift slow and easy under the calf's belly, letting it lay up against his hind legs, then just as he moved out I'd pull it up around his heels, holding the slack out of the rope and riding on. The calf would hit the ground stretched out nice and tight between those two ropes. It made branding a lot faster and a lot easier.

I just couldn't believe that Old Fooler had ever tried to kill me. He really enjoyed this branding and settled down and did his job just like the rest of us. The way he worked that rope was sweet as a baby's dream. He held it just tight enough but not too tight, and when you wanted slack he gave it to you. Those little short ears of his worked back and forth, and he watched every move out of those dark mean eyes. I still couldn't believe it when it was all over.

We turned the calves out to their mothers who were standing outside the corral. They trotted off together, all bawling, with the mother cows licking the calves like they had just been born.

I stared at Old Fooler standing out there looking so proud it showed right through the roan horsehair.

"I just can't figger that horse out," I said.

Wrangler said, "You never will. He's just like a woman."

"No," I said, "he may act like one but there is some little difference in the way they are built. How many mountain oysters we got."

"Enough," he said, "for a good supper."

We went to the house and washed up. I brought in some wood for the cookstove. Wrangler set about mixing up a bunch of batter to cook them calf balls in. I got out the jug Vince Moore had left and we took a big slug apiece.

I said, "Wrangler, maybe I'm gettin' the best of that Old Fooler horse after all."

He didn't answer.

I hunted up an old stub of a pencil and sat down at the table to see how much our bonus was. It was just too much to add up in my head.

"Let's see, eighteen mother cows and calves, three dry cows, and two steers." It took a lot of hard figuring, but I finally come up with the right answer.

I jumped up and took another slug out of the jug and yelled, "Wrangler, we've already made one hundred and fifteen dollars besides our regular wages."

"You don't mean it," he said, and sat down and figured it for himself. He never could get anything but a hundred and ten, but we decided as rich as we were that he was close enough.

I said, "Get back over to that stove. Them oysters is about to burn."

Pretty soon he took a pan of sourdough out of the oven browned just right. We poured us a big tin cup of coffee and sat down to consume a whole pan of crisp mountain oysters. It was the end of a hell of a fine day.

SIX

Everything was going along about as good as could be expected. We spent a lot of time, between runs on the mesa, trying to put a finish on some of the broncs. We kept three or four on a stake rope all the time. There is nothing better for a horse than that. Let an old pony get tangled up in that rope and peel all the hide from his hocks right down to the frog of his foot, and he learns not to fight a rope anymore. First he gets respect for it, then he overcomes his fear. If a horse won't work with a rope, he ain't fit for a thing.

I was teaching them to turn at the slightest pressure of the knee and the feet of the rein on their necks. If you have to turn a horse by force and pressure from the bits only, you are going to ruin his mouth. He will get high-headed and start slinging his head. That kind of horse is a disgrace to any cowboy. I like to train a horse to back, too. There are lots of places you get with a cow horse that you will need to back out of. Another thing we worked hard on was stopping. A horse should stop with his hind legs well up under his belly and his tail jammed almost in the ground. This way is lots smoother, and leaves both the horse and rider ready to turn and move out. He has to be trained this way to keep him from overworking the livestock. I put a good stop on them by throwing my weight back in the saddle just as I pull up on the reins.

Jim Ed was not only going to have a lot of lost cattle found and gathered, he was going to have a top string of cow ponies by the Fourth of July.

Now maybe that's going too far. There was one big exception— Old Fooler. The thought caused my gizzard to cloud over. I felt a lot better about him after the branding, but I knew if I got overconfident the son of a bitch would try to kill me again. Just the same, I caught myself feeling pleased with him.

We had penned just about all the mother cows and calves. Now the rough part was starting. Those old thousand-pound steers and big fat dry cows were wilder than outhouse rats. We had jumped one huge steer about ten times, but we never even got him bent down the mountain toward the flats, much less had a chance to fit a loop over them long sharp horns.

We were riding along tracking him. I was on Old Fooler. Wrangler was on his favorite black. We saw where he had gone into a big thicket of oak brush and topped out on a steep point.

I said, "Wrangler, he's still in there. You stay up on this point so I can skylight you and I'll mosey over on the other side and go in after him."

"Whatever suits you just tickles me plumb to death," he said.

"Now if he comes out where you can get a run at him," I went on, "just yell and I'll know what you mean. If he comes out where you can't, but I can, just point at the spot and I'll go after him like Jim Ed does to money."

I rode around and reined Old Fooler into the brush. He didn't like it but went in just the same. I heard something move. Then it sounded like a whole herd of hydrophobia buffalo had broke loose. It was just that one big steer.

I looked up and saw Wrangler pointing. He yelled, "To your left! There he goes!"

The steer had cut right back out not twenty feet away. I turned Old Fooler and that's all I had to do. Out of there he sailed with his head down and his ears laid back flat. I caught a glimpse of the steer and knew we had him going at an angle downhill. It was up to

Old Fooler now. He really put out. I could feel that smooth running power of his building up at every stride and pretty soon we could see that old steer's flying tail most of the time. Another half minute and I was actually thinking about undoing my rope and getting a loop ready. *Cowboys, what a horse!* I said to myself. I was sure glad Vince had brought him back. I was going to have to figure some way to trade Jim Ed out of this fine steer-gathering old pony.

Well, the steer hit a bunch of scattered piñons. I could see a big opening just past. I jobbed the steel to Old Fooler and he gave it all he had. Things were looking up. The next thing I knew I was too, but I couldn't see much.

We had started around this piñon tree, and I had leaned over just enough so Old Fooler would know which side to go on. He acted like he was doing just what I wanted, but when we got to the tree he whirled back the other way at full speed. So there I was trying to go around one side, and him going around the other. My chest whopped into hard bark and off I went.

I was laying on my back trying to find the sky. My breath was gone and every move I made I could feel them busted ribs scraping against one another. It hurt so bad I tried not to breathe at all. I reckon that's why old Wrangler thought I was dead when he first rode up. But he soon found out different because as bad hurt as I was I could still think up new names for that double-crossing Fooler horse.

As soon as Wrangler figured I had at least a fifty-fifty chance of living, he rode on down and gathered Old Fooler and led him back. I would have taken a piñon limb and beat him to death right then and there but it was all I could do to hold myself together long enough for Wrangler to help me up on him. I couldn't have picked up a broken matchstick at that moment.

It was a long ride in. I laid around in my bedroll for four or five days, moaning and groaning. Finally Wrangler took some strips of ducking canvas and tied them around me and it helped hold the ribs in place.

I asked him, "Ain't you got an old .44 pistol in your war bag?"

Wrangler looked at me out of them pig eyes and pulled at his drooping britches.

"Yeah," he said.

"Will it shoot?"

"I don't know," he said. "I never shot it."

"Well, let me see it," I said. I pulled the hammer back and shot right up through the ceiling. It went off like a wet firecracker.

"Wrangler," I said, "if you'll go down and shoot that son of a bitch I will give you all my bonus from this wild-cow gather."

"Naw," he said.

"Why not?" I asked.

"Hell, he belongs to Jim Ed and we'll have to pay for him. Jim Ed will charge us double and be makin' a big profit."

Well, this thought hurt me just as bad as that tree did. I couldn't stand for Jim Ed to profit by that horse's death instead of me.

"Wrangler," I said, "there are times you amaze me. You actually show faint signs of intelligence once in a while."

Wrangler did not think this was funny and he made a noise like a fat bay mule that has just jumped a five-wire fence.

"I am goin' to stay here and get well and then I am goin' to go out and kill him in the line of duty."

When Wrangler asked, "How?" I gave him the same kind of answer he'd given me.

When my ribs healed to where I could take a deep breath, I told Wrangler, "Get that horse up for me, will you?"

"What horse?"

"You know what horse," I said.

He brought Old Fooler up. I limped out and stood and stared. Then I brushed him down nice and gentle-like, taking my time. I talked as sweet to him as I would to my old crippled grandmother. I bragged on that horse and told him that if only I had any sugar cubes I would give him a whole sack. I mean to say, I spread it on like honey on a hot biscuit. Then I got on him and rode easy and slow out toward the hills, not even touching him with my spurs and still bragging on him like he was my favorite animal in all the world.

I got off up there a ways and my ribs was aching to beat hell, but they still held together. Then I ducked my head like I had just found a fresh track. It was at least two weeks old. Then I threw my head up and made out like I had spotted a thousand head of unbranded steers. I didn't have to do anything but lean over, and away we went. You could build a fire on a jackrabbit's tail and he would look like he was going backward compared to the way Old Fooler ran. I could almost feel that rascal laughing plumb through the saddle leather. What a fool he thought I was. This time he would really get me.

The ground was rolling away under us so fast it made me dizzy. Right out ahead was another bunch of piñon. I spurred him straight at them, leaning over just like I did before. Old Fooler was already bunching his muscles to jump the wrong way and break my crazy neck once and for all. Just as he thought it was time, I straightened up and pulled one foot out of the stirrup, yanking my leg up behind the cantle of the saddle. Then I jerked him into that tree at full speed.

There must be a lot more wind in a horse than in a man. The air that came busting out of his lungs would have blown a Stetson hat around the world three times. That old horse staggered and fell. I stepped off, taking care not to make any sudden movements and snap a rib. A cowboy in my condition has got to be careful and not take any chances.

I hadn't killed him, though. He got up, and his eyes were rolling around in his head like a couple of gallstones in a slop jar. He wobbled on his legs.

I fancy-stepped all the way back to camp with Old Fooler stumbling along behind, just barely able to make it. That was the only time I ever took a walk I enjoyed.

Wrangler came out on the porch and asked, "What happened?"

I said, "You know what? That is the tree-lovingest horse I ever saw. He just can't pass one by without runnin' over it."

I knew that I had cured that pony of at least one bad habit. It probably wouldn't do any good, though, as I figured he would die before morning.

I was wrong again. Not only did he get well in a couple of days, but he was doing better than I was. This made me so mad I decided to keep the lessons going. With a short piece of rope I necked Old Fooler to the biggest pack mule we had. Old Fooler didn't like this one bit. He looked at me with those dark, evil-thinking eyes of his and I could just feel ribs and bones snapping all over me.

It didn't make any difference. The mule led him off out into the pasture acting like he didn't even see Old Fooler coming along. That is one of the best ways a cowboy can use to gentle and teach a bronc to lead.

A couple of days later I was sitting on the porch having a smoke and wondering if my ribs would hold together for another set-to with the wild bunch on the mesa when up rides Onofre Martínez on a scraggly-looking bay. Old Onofre is a friend of mine. He has a little place over east of us a ways—twenty-five or thirty head of sheep, about ten cows, five goats, four hound dogs, and eight or ten kids.

"Howdy, Onofre, you old son of a gun. Get down and tie your horse," I said.

He got down and tied his horse to a post holding up the rickety porch.

"Hello, my friend," he said, sticking one dark paw out at me. "What are you doing down here?"

"Me and Wrangler are down here on a vacation," I said. "Good-hearted Jim Ed thought the north part of the JL would be too cold for a couple of tender-skinned boys like me and Wrangler."

"A considerate boss, this Jim Ed," said Onofre.

"Yeah," I said. "When is the last time you been into town?" Meaning the town of Hi Lo, New Mexico.

"Just last week, my friend," said Onofre. "Had a nice little pitch game over at Moon's Bar."

Onofre went on to tell me about the pitch game, then the poker game, then the big drunk, then how pretty his young sister was who lived in town. It made me nervous, all this talk. Then it made me thirsty. And hungry.

I said, "Onofre, how would you like a slug of some of Vince Moore's wonderful stuff?"

"I could think for days without conceiving a better thought," said Onofre.

I got the jug out. It was still half full.

"Where is Wrangler?" Onofre asked, wiping his mouth.

"He's up in the hills lookin' for cows."

"You boys must have done a good job already," said Onofre, motioning out into the gather pasture where the herd had grown pretty sizable.

"Not bad, Onofre. We get five dollars a head bonus."

"Calves and all?" he asked wide-eyed.

"Calves and all," I said.

"Whoooeee, there's goin' to be a big Fourth of July in Hi Lo, no?"

"Sí, hombre," I said.

We rattled on for a while, going over some of the good times we had had together, when I happened to think of Old Fooler. I was just going to light in and cuss him when I saw that mule leading him in toward the spring out by the corrals. They were coming slow but would make it in the next fifteen or twenty minutes. I started handing that jug to Onofre so fast he didn't hardly have time to get one swallow out of the way before another was right on its tail.

I got to looking at that sorry single-rig saddle of his. Now there is a big difference of opinion about the flank cinch on horses. I like a double-rig outfit because you can rope bigger stock without jerking your saddle off. When an old pony is really ducking his head and turning it on, it helps to have the rear end of your saddle tied down so it isn't whipping you in the rump at every jump. The other side thinks that with a single rig your horse won't do near as much bucking in the first place. All I know is, I always feel sorry for those single-rig boys. And them bits that Onofre had on his bridle— short-shanked and light as a gnat's whiskers. Just the kind of bit to ruin a horse. No wonder that little ugly bay of his had his head up in Onofre's face, slinging it around like a duck in a dry pond. He had iron stirrups instead of wooden. If a horse fell on him, those stirrups would more than likely bend over his foot and his horse would drag him to death. What a rig! I got to thinking that all this sorry equipment was just what Old Fooler deserved. I passed the jug to Onofre again.

After he'd lowered the jug for about the twentieth time he spotted Old Fooler and the mule. "What you got that roan horse necked to that mule for?"

It was exactly what I wanted him to ask.

"It's the other way around," I said. "That is the worst spoiled mule I ever saw—just kicks and tears up everything he gets close to. We have to keep him necked to Old Fooler all the time. He's the only thing around that can handle him."

"I be damned," said Onofre.

About that time the mule stuck his muzzle in the water and took a long pull. Old Fooler started to do the same. The mule ran backward bending hell out of Old Fooler's neck. The mule came back to drink. So did Fooler. The same thing happened. That mule simply was not going to let Old Fooler drink. I wondered what in the hell Old Fooler had done to that mule to make him so mad.

"Look," I said. "Look at that goddam mule. Ain't even goin' to let that good old roan horse have a drink of water. Now, ain't that the meanest damn mule you ever saw?"

"He sure is," said Onofre, swaying just a little and squinting his eyes to see better.

"I tell you what, Onofre, if you'll go pen them animals I'm goin' to turn that mule out to himself. That roan is the best horse on the whole outfit. We just can't take any more chances of the mule ruinin' him."

Onofre got up and climbed on his horse. He rode out and drove them in the corral.

I untied Old Fooler from the mule. He actually gave me a half-grateful look.

I saddled up Old Fooler and pointed out to Onofre how still he stood. How gentle he was. Onofre sagged against the corral, and agreed. Then I got up on him and rode him around the corral.

"Did you ever see a horse rein like this one?" I asked.

"That's the best I ever saw," said Onofre.

"Look what a stop he's got," I said, kicking Old Fooler into a run and leaning back and showing off his brakes.

"Never saw anything like it, my friend," said Onofre. "What you pulling so hard on that saddle horn for?" he asked.

"It's the rein he's got," I said. "So fast he might turn out from under me."

"Oh," said Onofre.

I got off, unsaddled, and led Old Fooler up to the house, watching every move. I didn't want to take any chances on him running off into the timber with me. Onofre followed, stumbling along, figuring this was the day for walking.

We sat down on the porch and I handed Onofre the jug. He really took a slug. That Adam's apple of his was jumping around like a barefooted kid in a red-ant bed. I helped myself to an outsized drink and said, "Onofre, ain't we always been the best of friends?"

"Sí, amigo."

"Ain't we played poker, fist-fought, run women, raised hell together?"

"Sí, sí, mi amigo. Sí, sí."

"Ain't you been just like a brother to me and me to you?"

"That is right, my friend," he said, reaching for the jug of wonderful stuff.

"There ain't nobody in the world that I have had more fun with, Onofre. Remember the time we got in jail over at Hi Lo for breaking up the poker game with them crooked Madison brothers?"

"How could I forget, my friend?" he said.

"Well, now, out of appreciation for all we've been through together and for this here long and everlasting friendship, I am goin' to do something for you."

Onofre was silent. He looked at me out of them big soft black eyes of his and waited, almost breaking into tears.

I said, jumping up and grabbing him by both shoulders, "Onofre, I'm goin' to make you the greatest gift one man can make another!"

The tears squirted out of his eyes at that, and if I hadn't been holding him up he would have fell on his face right on the ground.

"You goin' to kill yourself for me?" he asked.

"No, better than that," I said. "I am goin' to give you that beautiful roan horse. The greatest piece of horseflesh in New Mexico!"

Onofre just couldn't hold back any longer. The tears ran down his cheeks like a whitefaced cow taking a piss on a flat rock. He shook my hand until I thought it was a water pump.

"Gracias, my friend," he said. "My friend, my old amigo, my compadre."

"Now, get on your pony," I said, "and lead this here wonderful animal home to show your wife and kids."

I had to help him on his horse. All the time he was blubbering and telling the saints to send me straight to heaven without holding court over my soul. He rode out of there swaying in the breeze like a baby cottonwood.

A few days later me and Wrangler were out in the corral saddling some ponies, fixing to head for the hills. I was bragging about getting rid of Old Fooler once and for all.

I said, "If old Onofre can't ride him he will kill him and eat him, as many kids as he's got to feed."

I felt my horse throw his head up and look around. There was something coming toward the corral in a cloud of dust. It ran right up to the gate in a dead run and came to a sliding halt. That's right. It was Old Fooler. The saddle was up on his withers, and the one cinch was stretched like thin skin around a snakebite. The reins were broken off at the bits, and one of Onofre's boots was still dangling from a stirrup.

"Reckon Onofre's all right?" Wrangler asked.

"If he ain't, we'll hear about it in a few days," I said.

Wrangler said, "Wonder what happened?"

"Old Fooler just didn't like that sorry single riggin'," I said.

SEVEN

It might have been two or three degrees warmer at lower camp than it was at headquarters, but it was still colder than a well-digger's ass in Alaska. It wasn't because of the snow either. Down around the shack it would mix up with the sand and gravel and blow around in circles until it just plain evaporated. Up in the shade of the rimrocks you could sometimes find drifts two or three feet deep. The ground was frozen in the shade and it made tracking hard. The gather slowed down. We had to ride twice as far and rub saddle leather twice as long to get half as many head. The wind whistling around the mesa top was freezing cold and it never seemed to let up.

Me and Wrangler wore heavy sheep-lined coats. Just the same our eyes watered and our noses ran like leaky water troughs from the cold. The hair grew out long and shaggy on the horses and cattle. The wind bent and broke the dried-out grama grass. The stock got thinner and so did our horses.

At night the wind howled around that little old shack, shaking hell out of it and shoving that freezing cold through every crack. I kept thinking it was a long long time to the Fourth of July. I thought about Jim Ed and cussed him out to Wrangler, swearing that I was going to quit his chicken outfit in the spring.

We were sure as hell giving the broncs a workout up on those half-frozen slopes. They were gentling down fast, but like all horses in cold weather they had a tendency to want to buck a little when first saddled in the morning. We were used to this, but I never got used to Old Fooler. I was forced to saddle him once in a while, riding all the time with my guts right up in my throat and feeling that cold sensation in my belly that had nothing to do with the winter wind. I was beginning to wonder if my nerve was breaking on me and if that goddam horse would kill me before spring. I was just as nervous as a whore at a convention of Sunday-school teachers.

The winter wore on, and me and Wrangler sort of wore with it. Somehow, by staying on guard every single second, I had kept from getting hurt by Old Fooler for quite a spell. I kept thinking I should knock him in the head and get it over with, but at the same time I kept kidding myself into thinking I might win out.

The winter slacked up just a little. In the middle of the day, where the sun could hit, the ground thawed. It got to where we could do a little decent tracking again. I kept seeing the tracks of that big old outlawed steer, and something started eating at me. Seems like for a while I thought almost as much about catching that steer as I did about breaking Old Fooler. It was just about the same amount of problem. I jumped him out a half-dozen times by myself and with Wrangler along. He just showed us his tail and ran off, tearing hell out of the thick brush. It got kind of embarrassing.

"A couple of fine cowboys we are," I said to Wrangler.

"That steer is going to be the cause of me going to work in a gas station," said Wrangler.

Then I had an idea. Now most cowboys get the skull ache if they try to think overly much, but this was such a brand-new idea that I couldn't help but feel good about it.

"Wrangler," I said, "you know that Jim Ed told us to butcher whatever beef we needed to winter on."

"He did," said Wrangler.

"Well, I am goin' to shoot that goddam steer," I said, looking at Wrangler and expecting him to jump right through the side of the shack yelling, "Hooray for Hurrah!"

He looked at me, pulled his britches almost up on his hips,

snorted through his busted nose, and said, "Hell's bells, no better than you can shoot, you'll never get close enough to hit the same mountain he's on."

"Bullshit carver!" I said. "Without a rope hangin' and draggin' me back in the brush I can spur right on up to him."

"Maybe you could on Old Fooler," he said, looking way off out the one little dirty pane left in the west window.

I never said a word. I just walked over and got Wrangler's six-shooter out of his war bag and went out and gathered in the horses. Old Fooler kept rolling his eyes around, half expecting me to fit a loop around his wicked neck. Somehow there was a gleam in his eye that made my loop sail over him and settle gentle-like over the neck of the big bay that had turned out so good. It was the horse I knew Jim Ed would pick out for his own. It wasn't very long till I had him saddled. I turned the other horses out and rode for the hills.

It was cold but warming some as the sun moved toward the middle of the sky. My heavy sheepskin coat was breaking the wind pretty good except for a few leaks around the collar and sleeves. My breath was frosting out in front of me and the bay's was doing the same.

I rode up and around through the open spots looking for the steers tracks. I didn't find them. That six-shooter was setting there in my coat pocket all loaded and ready to go. I was about to give up when I felt the bay bunch up under me and throw his head up and his ears forward. Right across a little draw stood the big red steer. He snorted and whirled, heading for some oakbrush a quarter-mile to the north. I leaned over on the bay and he lit out of there in a dead run. The wind was blowing to our backs, but it was left far behind. I didn't feel it at all.

That bay was a natural-born cow horse. He judged just the angle to cut that steer out of the brush. It was close all right, but just the same we headed him back and down through a bunch of piñons. Well, I leaned over as low as I could in the saddle to duck all those low-hanging limbs and jobbed the steel in the bay's sides. We moved up fast.

Pretty soon I could see a glimpse of the steer at every jump. Then we hit this clearing going what seemed like about ninety miles an hour. I hit the bay again with the spurs, letting out a yell and pulling the pistol out of my pocket at the same time. The hammer got kind of hung in my pocket lining, and it looked like the steer would make it to the brush before I could get a shot in. I finally got the damned gun out and there we were, right on top of the steer. I pulled the trigger. Then me and the bay were rolling through that clean, pure, fresh mountain air. Down we went. The world sure did seem big and hard where we hit. It jumped around for a while. Then it settled down to where I could see. I was flat on my back, and eleven hundred pounds of horseflesh was laying on both my legs almost up to my knees. That horseflesh wasn't moving. I had blown that bay horse's brains right out his ears. The very bay horse that I knew my boss, Jim Ed Love, wanted for his very own.

I strained, I pulled, I pushed, I clawed at the ground like a fat tomcat with the thin dirties. I couldn't budge an inch from under that horse. I cussed. I prayed. I rolled and moaned. It just didn't do any good. I was stuck. Pretty soon the sun would set and it was going to get plenty cold. If I stopped moving I would freeze. I wondered how long it would be before Wrangler missed me and came looking. There was an awful lot of country I could be in besides where I was.

It was not a nice place to be. I was ashamed to be found in such a position even if I died. It took about four or five days for the sun to set. The cockeyed coyotes started howling. I always kind of liked to hear this noise before, but now it was an unpleasant sound. I could see a lot of stars up above but I didn't consider them very pretty. I kept moving my arms and tried not to think about sleep. I knew damn well I had to stay awake and moving or else join a lot of other good cowboys in another camp. I didn't know what time of night it was, but a hell of a lot of owls had hooted and gone to roost.

For a minute or two I was sort of discouraged with the carefree life of a cowboy. What had ever made me take up this calling anyway, that could put a man out here by himself in the mountains on a cold winter night with a dead horse for a blanket?

Seems like the first thing I could remember was Pa leading me around on an old ranch horse of his called Shorty. I wasn't old enough to go to the toilet by myself but I was old enough to get up on that horse. I reckon that's what you call being born in the saddle. A few years later I remember Pa telling me I looked like a big fat washwoman the way I was getting on my horse.

"Look here," he said, "get that mane and reins in your left hand and the reins and the saddle horn in your right and stick your left knee in that horse's shoulder. This way he's got to turn toward you when he moves out—otherwise he'll turn away from you and kick your belly button off."

Later on: "Good Lord, boy, don't you know better than to put your spur buckles on the inside of your boots? You're really asking for trouble that way. Keep them buckles on the outside so they can't get hung in the riggin'. . . . Look at that leather thong holdin' the top of your chaps together. Why, that's way too strong. What if you was to get throwed up over the saddle horn and that leather wouldn't break? Why, that horse would buck you to death. . . . Here, boy, don't never get on a horse without untracking him. You can tell a whole lot about what mood a horse is in just by untracking him. . . ."

Day after day, year after year, it seemed like all I got was an ass-chewing.

"Here, boy, you gone crazy? Don't never get down off a horse when he's drinkin'. He'll run backward with you every time. Keep your left trigger finger between the reins. You can handle a horse better that way and have the feel of every move he makes . . . Man alive, boy, you are goin' to lose your catch rope. Don't you know to never put less than three wraps around your rope with the horn string? If you don't, your rope will come loose and fall under your horse."

It never let up.

Then I remembered one morning in particular when I was riding with Pa. It was a good day. We had plenty of rain on our little two-by-four outfit. The green grass was pushing up out of the ground thick and fast. The cows were full and lay around in the sun chewing their cuds. The tongue marks in their thick hair showed they had been licking themselves—a sure sign they were doing good.

The calves reminded me of a bunch of kittens, the way they jumped around playing. Their faces were clean and pure white compared to the darker, grass-stained ones of the mother cows.

Out of pure habit, Pa counted the cows and said, "That ole muley cow, the one that went dry, is missin'."

I looked at him and said, "Maybe she's in the bog."

"No, it ain't likely," Pa said, "since we fixed that good pole fence around it."

"Yeah," I said, "but you know how that old black cow was we used to have? She'd tear down the fence just to get hung up in the bog."

"Well, we'll ride over and see," Pa said.

Riding over to look at the bog I was feeling kind of proud of Pa in spite of all the eating-outs he had given me, and I was remembering some of the things he had taught me.

I had finally learned when driving a bunch of cows to tell if one really meant to bolt the herd or was just running a bluff. This saves lots of wear and tear on both horses and cowboys.

I knew when unsaddling a horse to always undo the flank cinch first. Otherwise I might forget and pull the saddle off with the flank cinch still buckled. When that happens a horse was sure to buck and kick the saddle to pieces. I knew that a horse should work with his head down close to his withers for best results. A high-headed horse blocks a cowboy's view and is a shame on any working cow ranch. I had been taught all this and a hell of a lot more.

"Look, Pa," I yelled, "I told you that old cow was in the bog."

We pulled out to where she had knocked the poles down. The cow was struggling deep in the mud, sinking inch by inch as she strained.

"Now, don't that beat you," said Pa. "All this green grass out here and the old son of a bitch breaks in there to get a bite of grass she ain't supposed to have."

Pa took down his rope and spurred up as close as he could, just out of the mud. He tied one end to the saddle horn and took the coils in his left hand and the loop in his right.

"Sure wish she had horns," he said. "This is goin' to be rough on the old fool. I'll have to rope her around the neck, and that's goin' to choke her."

Pa whirled the loop. It floated out and circled around the cow's neck. He jerked the slack and spurred old Shorty away from the bog. The rope tightened. Shorty lowered his head and lunged against the rope. Still the old cow was stuck tighter than a new boot on a bigfooted kid. Her eyes bulged as the rope putted tighter. Shorty hit the rope again, hard and steady.

The old muley cow struggled. Her breath was grinding in bursts out her nostrils. Then she was out six inches, then to her belly, then her hocks. At last she was on dry ground.

I spurred up and threw a loop at her heels. I missed.

Pa turned back, dragging the cow, and yelled at me: "Here now, boy, use a slow loop. A fast loop is no good for heelin', except in a rodeo arena."

The next time I caught. We spurred in opposite directions. The old cow stretched out flat on the ground. Pa rode up to give the rope slack around her neck. I kept mine tight. Pa jumped down and took the rope off the cow's neck. He yelled, "Give me slack, boy!" I spurred up. He jerked the rope off the cow's heels. She got up and made a run at Pa before he could get to his horse. But I was watching and rode between them, heading her out toward the rest of the herd.

We fixed the pole up and rode back toward the ranch house with me wondering why that old cow was so mad because we had saved her life.

Well sir, while I was laying there thinking back about these things and telling myself what a fool I had been to ever learn anything at all about horses, the night wore on. But it didn't warm up any. My arms were getting kind of tired from slinging them around, and it seemed like from my ass down I was already froze solid to the ground.

It might have been all right just to be a plain old cowboy, but to be a horse breaker along with it was the sad mistake. If I hadn't of showed off back there on the Diamond-2 that day when I was just a big-butted kid, maybe it would have been easier.

An old blue horse had unloaded Cliff Hadley, the top rider for the Diamond-2. He came limping back up to the corrals where the blue stood and waited for him. It was sure griping Cliff to take that walk. Besides, we all stood and watched him coming. Finally he got close enough so we could hear him talking.

"Lead that son of a bitch out in the corral. I'm goin' to feed him a bellyful of steel." Hadley didn't last past the third jump. The blue went up, turned sideways, and sucked back in a spine-twisting, gut-jarring leap that drove Cliff face first into the corral dust. Now, Cliff was a bronc rider and he got right back on. First his hat went, then he lost a stirrup, then off he sailed again, whomping into the ground like a sack of wet meal.

"When a horse can buck my hat off, cain't no man ride him," he said.

Well, I just couldn't help but have a try at it. At first the blue walked around easy and gentle-like, reining good—something like Old Fooler. Then he ducked his head low, squealed like a schoolgirl running through the brush, and leaped right straight up with all four legs in the air. He came down with his legs like four wooden stilts. The jar loosened every bone in my body. The next jump my hat went, then a stirrup. I was pulling that saddle horn out by the roots. Somehow I got the stirrup back. Then he flew high and to the right, and as his front legs hit the ground his hind end swung around in an arc. Then he went into a long straight forward leap, kicking back hard. At every kick I felt my head snap back. I was sure my neck was broke in at least ten places. I held on to the horn, jamming my right elbow down over my right hipbone. Just as I knew my insides were squeezing out between my ribs and every joint was ground to powder, I felt him weaken. The blue was squealing like a dying rabbit and all I could see was a flash of mane and I was thinking that I was setting right up on the tip end of a blue tornado.

He hadn't weakened much. Everything started looking gray as my head was flung back harder and harder. I didn't know it right then, but a long streamer of bright red was running down out of my nose and across my shoulder. Then the blue roan slowed fast. With all my might I swung the spurs out and into his belly. He was slowing and I was sitting solid in the saddle. I could see his neck now and out of the corner of my eyes the corrals and the cowboys standing there yelling. Then it was over.

I crawled down all weak and wobbly but I tried not to let anybody know it. The blue roan was plumb black with sweat and stood spread-legged with his head down, breathing hard. He was beat.

When the boys began to tell me what a ride I'd made I said, feeling kind of smart-like, "All you got to do is keep them between your legs."

Well, I've only got hold of one horse since that could buck as hard—another roan it was. That bastard of an Old Fooler is the one I mean. From that day on, the word spread and I always drew the rough string. Oh, for the life of a cowboy!

It seemed like it had been around two or three years since that bay had rolled on top of me. I wiggled my arms and hands every once in a while. There wasn't a whole lot of feeling left in them.

The stars were gone and over there somewhere the sun was making a stab at coming up. If I could just last till it got high enough to thaw me out, Old Wrangler might accidentally find me. There wasn't much of a chance, but it was all I had to keep me company.

Well, the sun came up and I couldn't hold my eyes open any longer. I just let them shut and away I went. It was late that afternoon when Old Wrangler found me. He was riding his favorite black and leading Old Fooler. It had been Old Fooler that had thrown his head up and kept looking through the thick brush toward the opening where I was taking it easy. Wrangler told me all this later while he was tying a splint around my right leg. He made it from some boards out of the floor of our shack. But when he woke me up and told me he was going to drag that bay off me, all I could see was the horse he had brought for me to ride home on.

"Why, you dirty bastard," I said, "if you ain't a good friend bringin' that outlawed son of a bitch with you. Hell's fire, just leave me here!"

EIGHT

I kept that busted leg propped up in front of the fire most of the time. It had been about ten days since Wrangler had tied the splints around it. A piece of cowhide covered the hole in the floor where he had torn up the boards to make the splints. I was setting there looking at that hide, thinking that old Wrangler was having all the fun. He had gathered three dry cows and a lone yearling all by himself since I got fouled up.

"Wrangler," I said, "do you reckon Jim Ed will take it out of my pay for shooting that bay horse?"

"You know goddam well he will," Wrangler answered.

"If he does I'm goin' to tell him to go to hell with a downhill run. I'm goin' to quit the JL and go get me a job wranglin' dudes," I said.

"You better think a long time about that," said Wrangler.

"About what?" I asked.

"About wranglin' dudes. Remember what happened to me?"

"Yeah," I said, "that is right. Well then, maybe I can do like you said you was gonna do. Get me a job in a gas station."

Setting around with this busted leg gave me the gripes, so I lit in on Jim Ed.

"Now, Wrangler, I think I *will* quit this outfit, anyway. All the other hands got to make the fall roundup. We didn't. They ride the gentle, easy workin' horses me and you break out. And what do we ride?" I asked. "Nothing but the rough string. I can't remember when I've rode anything but a bunch of outlawed horses."

"That's the way it is," Wrangler said.

"I bet you the other hands have been into town two or three times a month, and here we set down here a half mile from hell and thirty-five miles from town. It just ain't right," I griped. "Now, it ain't long till Christmas. Ever'body else will be in Hi Lo havin' a big turkey dinner and passin' out presents and havin' themselves a sure-enough fine time. Do you think Jim Ed Love will give a damn about us settin' off down here all by ourselves? Hell, no! Then New Year's there'll be a big dance and lots of good music to go with it. I bet Jim Ed gives all the rest of the hands a whole week off."

"Yep," said Wrangler.

"Besides," I went on, "that Jim Ed Love is the meanest bastard in nine counties. I'll bet half my wages he charges me forty dollars for that bay horse."

"More than that, I reckon," said Wrangler.

I wished Wrangler hadn't of said that. It upset me somewhat. "Well, if he does he just lost a horse breaker for good. Can you imagine a man that would charge a cowboy for killin' a horse in the line of duty?"

"Well," said Wrangler, "there ain't many cowboys kills a good, well-broke horse by shootin' his brains out in a dead run."

I reached for a piece of stove-wood, planning to knock Wrangler in the head. Then I got to thinking about what a good cook he was and let it go.

"This is the coldest goddam winter I ever saw," I said. "And the longest. Seems to me like we been down here for a whole year already."

"Been quite a spell," said Wrangler, and shoved a pan of sourdough in the oven.

"I had rather live like a blanket-ass Indian than the way we are livin'," I said.

"Did I ever tell you that I was part Indian?" asked Wrangler, setting down and rolling a Bull Durham.

I could see he was about to go over his two-grunt and one-sentence limit. "Everybody I ever talked to," I said, "claims to be part Indian."

"Them Indians gets around," he said. "It was my grandpa that was full-blood," he added.

"How much does that make you?" I asked.

"I don't know," he said. "I have tried to figure it fifty times but it's just too much addin' and subtractin' for me. He was married to a squaw as big and fat as that Toy Smith woman I was tellin' you about. Seems like us Lewis folks always draw fat women. You think this is a cold winter," Wrangler said. "Let me tell you about the one my grandpa spent in Montana."

I could tell Old Wrangler was fixing to bear down on some wild-eyed story. So I looked up like I just couldn't wait to hear it.

"Grandpa was just a young buck then. A hunter. It was in a February, and Grandpa, two more bucks, and a squaw was camped out huntin' game for the rest of the tribe. Grandpa said this buck's squaw was a way fatter than his old woman. In fact, he said she was the fattest woman he ever saw. The reason was that she was an expert skinner—they had her along to skin the animals—and she was always sneaking tastes of raw meat. Claimed she could tell if it was goin' to make good jerky or not that way. She and her Indian was in one tepee and Grandpa and the other Indians was in another."

Wrangler was really warming up now. "Talk about a winter. They hadn't no sooner got set than the snow commenced to fall. It set in and snowed two foot the first day and it never stopped. Pretty soon they had eaten up all the grub they had brought along and they commenced to get a little lank in the middle. It just kept gettin' worse. Grandpa said his belly was as thin as a well-honed knife blade and it looked like they were done for.

"Finally they got to thinkin' about that fat squaw over in the other tepee. Ever' once in a while they would break out and go over and take a look at her. The snow was so deep they could climb right up and look down in the tepee from the top. Grandpa said that old squaw was sure doing good. She was like a hibernatin' bear— enough fat to last her a long time.

"Now her buck was in bad shape but he thought a lot of this squaw. After Grandpa spent about thirty minutes just lookin' down in that tepee with his mouth waterin', the buck looked up and saw him. He decided to slip his squaw out of camp, snow or no snow. Grandpa and the other buck were watchin', though, and they hadn't hardly left when Grandpa was after them. It was hard goin' in all that fresh snow, and they were so weak they could hardly walk."

"Did they catch 'em?" I asked, getting pretty interested in the outcome of this story about Wrangler's ancestors.

"Well," said Wrangler, "you see, the squaw's husband was just as weak as Grandpa, and the squaw wouldn't walk off and leave him."

"Yeah, but what I want to know is, did they catch 'em?"

"Wait a minute," said Wrangler. "Let me tell you. Grandpa and his runnin' mates took a shortcut, figgerin' just about where they would come together."

I couldn't wait any longer if I had to get up and throw Wrangler through the wall. "Goddammit, did they *catch* 'em?"

"Yeah, they sure did," he said. "Grandpa had figgered it just right. They all met in a little openin' with a lot of thick brush all around for a wind-break."

"What happened then?" I asked, feeling my sore leg starting to pound.

"Well, I don't rightly know. Grandpa wouldn't talk much about it but he did say that four sets of tracks came together in the fresh snow, and a few days later only three walked away."

"Oh," I said, feeling in the stomach something like I did every time I climbed on Old Fooler's back and also realizing that this present winter was a lot warmer than I'd thought.

"Wrangler, do you reckon if I was to catch that big red steer that Jim Ed might not charge me for killin' that bay horse?"

"Somethin' to study about," Wrangler said, not helping a bit.

"Why, that steer must weigh in the neighborhood of a thousand pounds," I said. "That's a lot of beef on the hoof."

I had already settled my mind to the fact that if I was going to catch that steer it would have to be on Old Fooler. It was an uneasy thought to live with.

Well, I sat around the fire and griped for a couple of more weeks. Christmas Day came around and we didn't have a decorated tree. We had run through them trees after wild stock until we couldn't stand the thought of having one in the house. But old Wrangler did the best he could. He took some dried apricots and cooked up the best-tasting pudding you ever wrapped your gums around. We butchered a beef and had us some steaks as thick as a two-by-four. It was all mighty good. We didn't give each other presents and we didn't sing carols, but we crawled in our bedrolls pretty well pleased all the same.

On New Year's Eve I couldn't sleep at all. Seems like I kept hearing that music all the way from Hi Lo, and I cussed Jim Ed till almost sunup.

My leg felt pretty good now, and I couldn't stand it any longer. Like I said, Wrangler was having all the fun. He was up in the hills somewhere when I took the splint off. It wasn't bad. I got Old Fooler up and decided I would take a ride out on the flats instead of up in the rocky country where he might fall on me.

I wasn't a mile from the shack when I saw this coyote watching me from behind a soapweed. Them two ears of his was sticking up like the back sights on a thirty-thirty. I rode along easy, keeping an eye on Old Fooler and the coyote both. I made out like I didn't see the coyote and kept riding in a circle—getting closer all the time. I had tried all my life to rope a coyote horseback but had never been on a horse fast enough to give him a loop. Once I almost caught one right after he gorged himself on a dead cow. He was so full I figured I would have caught him except that my horse stepped in a prairie-dog hole and rolled over about nine times. When I got to where I could see, the coyote was gone.

I started breathing harder the closer we got. Then all of a sudden I reined Old Fooler straight at him. I had already slipped the leather thong from around my rope. The coyote took off in a hard run, and Old Fooler really lit out after him. I shook a small loop out, knowing I would never be able to jerk the slack on a big one. The coyote was headed for some malpais breaks about a mile to the north and we were right on his tail.

For a while I didn't think Old Fooler was gaining; then I saw the coyote start switching his tail from side to side. That meant he was putting out all he had. Old Fooler must have known it too, because he laid his ears back and ran like a greyhound.

I could see them malpais breaks getting closer every heartbeat, and Old Fooler was gaining all the time. Then I could see the coyote glancing back and I whomped the spurs into Old Fooler's belly and there we were. This was it! There wouldn't be another chance. I leaned over and whipped that twine out and I saw the little loop lay right over that coyote's ears and across his nose. The coyote slung his head—and he was caught like a horse thief at a public hanging!

I rode right on by, and that coyote must have thought he was a big-ass bird because he sure did fly through the air. It wasn't near over yet. I still had to keep Old Fooler from taking off when I got down to kill the coyote. He sure surprised me. He worked that rope like a regular roping horse. I went up and took hold of the rope about three feet from the coyote and whirled him around in the air; then I brought him down hard. It didn't take but a minute more to stomp a boot heel into his ribs, and *that* coyote would never steal another chicken.

Old Fooler was snorting and raring back on the rope but he stayed put. I think the son of a bitch enjoyed it more than I did. For a minute, before I had time to reflect, I was real proud of Old Fooler. He had helped me do something I had wanted to do all my life. Something I had just about given up on.

Three or four days later I was riding Old Fooler along with Wrangler. We had just hit the foothills and I was bragging about catching that coyote. Wrangler wasn't saying word one. I'm not even sure he was listening.

Now, it ain't very often that a man can brag on a horse like Fooler. I had just said, "Wrangler, he worked that rope like the gentlest kid pony you ever saw. He may come out of it yet. What do you think?"

Wrangler just humped up in the saddle and grunted. This was not his day for talking.

"Yes sir, wouldn't that be something if Old Fooler gentled down and turned into a lady's horse after all?"

About the time I said this a big bobcat jumped up out of a little clump of brush and loped across a clearing. You hardly ever see a bobcat in the daytime and you hardly see a cowboy try to rope one. But after the coyote I was what town folks call "flushed with victory." If I was going to be hung on my wedding day, I couldn't have helped myself. Undone came that rope. Untracked came Old Fooler. A bobcat ain't half as fast as a coyote. It wasn't ten jumps till Old Fooler had me right on him. Fellers, it was easy. I was getting to be quite a roper. I never saw a loop fit around anything so clean in all my life. Just like the coyote. I rode right on by him, spurring to beat hell.

Well, I learned one new thing then and there. A bobcat's neck is made out of rubber. When that cat hit the end of the rope he went up in the air all right, but it was straight at Old Fooler's hindquarters. He was yowling to beat hell and he must have sunk them claws plumb to the bone in Old Fooler's hind end because that horse snorted and started bawling and bucking at the same time. I never had much chance after that to check up on the bobcat. It was all I could do to stay on Old Fooler. He took off through the brush, then bucked through the middle of a bed of sharp rocks. He was looking for a big hole to jump in, and he didn't care where he found it. I figured right then that if I ever wanted to teach a bunch of rodeo horses to buck, I would hire me a pen full of bobcats to train them. There wouldn't be enough riders left in a month to put on a show anywhere.

The next thing I knew I felt something digging in my back. It felt like an eagle with claws six inches long, but it was that bobcat. I couldn't turn loose of the saddle horn to knock him off, and if I did I wasn't sure I could get the job done. About that time Old Fooler ran under a low-hanging limb. I didn't see this limb. I don't know if the bobcat did or not. I never had a chance to ask him because Old Fooler just kept going with that rope stringing out behind and that bobcat meowing on the other end. I kind of sat up and waited for the world to come to an end. About that time Wrangler spurred by. He was after Old Fooler, but it looked to me like he was going to laugh himself to death before he caught him.

I sat down, rolled a smoke, and waited. I could still hear the brush crackling and Wrangler hee-hawing up the other side of the mountain. I failed to see what was so goddam comical.

About half an hour later Wrangler came back. He was leading Old Fooler. That horse was in one hell of a shape. He was brush-marked all over, and that bobcat had dug furrows in his hind end that looked like a fresh-plowed field. It took some time to find out how Wrangler had caught him so quick. Every time he would start to tell me he would slap those little old chap-covered bowlegs of his and just plain howl with laughter. It was a disgrace the way he carried on.

Finally, though, he told me. "Old Fooler ran that rope through a big forked stump. The fork was too narrow for the bobcat to get through."

"Oh," I said. "Didn't you bring the hide back with you? A bobcat hide is worth about ten dollars."

"Not this bobcat hide," he said. "There ain't a place on it the daylight wouldn't show through."

Well, we went on trying to gather more cattle. They were getting few and far between now. The wind was still blowing, but it wasn't near as cold. The drifts had started melting up around the rimrocks. And every once in a while in an out-of-the-wind spot we could see a few sprigs of green grass. The stock had scattered out all over hell trying to run down a decent bite or two. It made it hard to find them.

One day I was mounted on Old Fooler and riding by myself. Somehow me and Wrangler had got separated while tracking through the rocks. It was snowing a wet, cold snow up high, but down in the lower breaks it was drizzling a fine rain. I was really hunting for the big red steer, hoping I might make up for killing that good bay horse. I couldn't hardly stand the thought of all the ribbing I was going to get about that.

Then I jumped him—or rather Old Fooler jumped him. I felt him leap out and I thought, *Here we go again*. While I was gathering in the saddle horn I saw that Old Fooler had headed the steer downhill and that there wasn't anything but a few little patches of cedar between us and the flats. Now, I want to say here and now that I have rode some fairly rough country and some damn fast horses, but the way Old Fooler built to that steer would have made the greatest racehorse man in the world just jump right straight up and holler till he keeled over in a dead faint.

I got that rope down and shook me out a great big Mother Hubbard loop and it wasn't but a minute till I was almost close enough to throw. That loop looked like it never would settle down, but when it did that steer was in it!

I'd waited a long time for this. I put them spurs to Old Fooler and he went by that steer like it was standing still. I threw a trip on the way by. That is, I pitched the rope over on the steer's right side, wrapped it around and under his tail. When the slack came out of the rope with all of us going at full speed, there was a stack-up to remember. That steer was whipped around and up. When he came down it looked like he was trying to go to China headfirst. He got up shaking his head and turned back for the hills. Me and Old Fooler repeated the performance twice more. By then that steer was ready to go horn the devil, but he sure didn't want any more trouble out of *us*. We headed him for the gathering pasture at lower camp in a long trot with the catch rope still tied between us.

Now I was really proud of Old Fooler. I was a little proud of the way I had been roping lately, too. Sometimes you go for a month and no matter how hard you try, you just can't make that loop fit over anything. Either a figure eight comes in your loop or you hang it on a limb or just plain miss. But the last few times I'd thrown it, something would run its head into the circle.

It was a great day. Now maybe old Jim Ed wouldn't be so mad over me killing that bay horse. The rain was getting heavier. The lightning and thunder were really mixing it up. The ground turned slick as owl grease and shone like a big mirror every time the lightning flashed. That old steer was running along out ahead of us with his head down, his tongue lolled out to one side, slobbering like a mad dog. Me and Old Fooler came sliding along behind. *Let 'er rain*, I thought.

Finally we hit the gathering pasture fence and were only about a quarter of a mile from the gate. I was feeling mighty good. Then one of them bolts of lightning knifed down and hit the fence right between us and the steer. Blue sparks shot out in every direction, and when they bounced off my boots it felt like my legs had been pulled out by the roots. The steer went down, Fooler went down, and I went down with him. I was dizzy as hell but managed to stand up.

For a minute I thought Old Fooler was dead, but when I kicked him in the side he struggled to his feet. The wires along the fence were melted in two, and one post was black and splintered. That steer's horns were split like a drunk lumberjack had been swinging at them with a chopping ax. He was stone dead.

It was a long wet ride into lower camp, even if it was just three-quarters of a mile. But as the feller said in the song, "Spring is just around the corner."

NINE

The green grass came up in bigger patches. The wild stock up in the hills was pretty thin, and they ran off a lot more weight chasing after the green stuff. A really hard blizzard this time of year could have killed a lot of cattle, but it didn't come. What we had caught and held down in the gathering pasture was in good shape. The thick cured grass in the subirrigated pasture had kept them in the winter, and there was lots of green stuff mixed with it now. The long hair was shedding off in patches. The horses were shed off almost slick and had begun to pick up weight.

The snowbanks up high melted during the day and became smaller all the time. Me and Wrangler had rode all day without jumping a thing. We were still about five miles from camp when we stopped to water our horses at a big spring. I kept spurring Old Fooler up to the edge and he kept running backward. It had been a long hard ride and I just knew the old rascal was thirsty.

"What in the hell is the matter with you now?" I said as I jabbed at him again.

Wrangler's horse had his head down drinking long and deep. I hit Old Fooler with the spurs again. Now, this spring was still iced over just a little bit from the cold nights. Old Fooler let out a snort you could have heard all the way to Hi Lo, and jumped right out into the middle of the pond. I have had horses do a lot of things with me, but this was something new.

He went under and I went under with him. Then I came up and he came up, choking and strangling. He went down again. By then I was out of the saddle but still holding onto the saddle horn. The third time he went down I quit him. If I was going to drown I was going to do it my own way. Old Fooler came pawing at the thin ice and snorting water out of both nostrils. It looked like a windmill with twin pipes running wide open in a high wind. There was only one thing wrong. I can't swim. I kept going down and coming up, pawing just like Old Fooler at the thin edge of ice. It kept breaking off. I thought, *What a hell of a way for a cowboy to cash in his chips.*

Then Wrangler roped me. It was not a clean loop. It went around my neck and down under one arm. He turned around and spurred off like he was trying to jerk down a yearling bull. I came out of there like a catfish hooked right in the jaw. He drug me a ways before he turned around and let some slack in the rope.

I yelled, "God a'mighty, stop! I'd rather drown than be drug to death!"

Now, spring was easing up on us, but the middle of it was not here yet. That ride home that evening after the sun had set was not one of great comfort. The wind wasn't blowing too hard, but as wet as I was I could have felt the breath of a prairie dog from twenty feet underground.

I said, "Well, this son of a bitch has now tried everything in the world to kill me. He has run through corrals, barbwire fences, jumped off a bluff, rolled over me, kicked me in the belly, bit me in the back, run me into a tree, bucked me off and left me afoot, and now he's tried to drown me! You know what I am goin' to do to this dirty bastard, Wrangler? I am goin' to take him into town and sell him to a soap factory. Then I am goin' to buy the first bar of soap they make out of him. I am goin' to waller around in cow-shit for a week. Then I am goin' to bathe with that dirty son of a bitch. And ever' time I wash my hands from then on I am goin' to laugh like hell. That's what I'm goin' to do."

By the time we got into camp my clothes was froze so stiff I couldn't hardly get off of Old Fooler. I walked up to the house as stiff-legged as a man with the jake-leg. I had not enjoyed the afternoon, and I meant what I said about selling that terrible horse to a soap factory. If I had to go to work for the company myself.

When I was about half thawed out, Wrangler asked a stupid question. "How you feelin'?" he asked.

I said, "I feel just like that old boy that had been sleepin' out under the chuck wagon durin' a rainy spell: 'I am tired, wet, and hungry, busted, disgusted, and can't be trusted.'" There was more to this but Wrangler don't hold with dirty words.

It was hard to believe, but spring did come. Everything turned green and started growing. The does was having fawns, the coyotes was having pups, the cows was having calves, and me and Wrangler was about to start having fits if the Fourth of July didn't hurry and roll around. We gathered the winter's catch in and branded all the new calves. Then we counted our gather. A hundred head in all! Lord-a-mercy, a five-hundred-dollar bonus and all that back pay coming!

"Wrangler, we will go to town and celebrate gettin' rid of Old Fooler for a month," I said.

"That horse belongs to Jim Ed Love," Wrangler said, lowering my spirits.

"I will buy him if it takes half of what I've got," I said.

"You cain't let him know you want him," said Wrangler. "If the cheap bastard knew that, there ain't enough money in New Mexico could buy him."

"I won't let him know," I said. At the same time I was wondering how I was going to explain about shooting that bay horse.

Everything seemed to be coming out of the ground, even the snakes. I was riding out among our gather on a little sorrel gelding when he snorted and jumped sideways. It was a rattlesnake. He was behaving kind of funny. Then I saw what was going on. There was a rat squatting, paralyzed, not six inches from his hole in the ground. That snake was looking him straight in the eye. The rat wasn't moving. He was hypnotized.

At first I didn't think the snake was moving either. Then I saw he was. You couldn't actually see it—it was like the way the wind blows. You can feel it but can't see it. After a long time he was real near the rat. Then with a quick dart he had him. That rat came unhypnotized long enough to make one squeak, and that was all.

I got down and picked up a big stick. The snake dropped the dead rat and coiled, sticking that little black forked tongue in and out at me, and shaking his tail a mile a minute. I had a hard time holding my horse and killing that snake at the same time, but I did.

I rode on down to the pasture. One big old cow stood with her head down, her jaw swelled twice its regular size. That snake had bit her. She was breathing hard in the warm June sun, and I knew if I didn't do something quick the swelling would choke her to death. I fit a loop around her horns, got down and pulled out my knife. That old cow made one run sideways against the rope and then stopped. Seems like she knew she was a goner if I didn't do something for her. I opened the knife blade wide. Then I cut deep. The blood spurted out all green and black. By the time I got the rope off her the blood was running red and I knew she would live. Not everything that comes up in the spring is all to the good, I decided.

I rode on out and made another count of the cattle. The little calves were getting plenty of milk from their mothers and were gaining weight and feeling good. I reckon the prettiest sight in the world is a young calf when its mother is giving lots of milk. As long as me and Wrangler had been away from town, though, I imagine a woman would have run a mighty close contest with the calves. Any woman!

It was getting to where I couldn't hardly sleep at night for thinking about it. And lots of times while I lay awake in my bedroll I could hear Wrangler murmuring, "Irene. Irene." That little potbellied bastard had never told me about any Irene. I never asked him, either, because that was probably the one he had really cared about.

Well, it didn't get any better. I was craving to get into town so bad I could feel it plumb to my toenails. I wanted me and Wrangler to get bathed and shaved, get us some women, get drunk, get in the rodeo on the Fourth, and last but not even close to least, get that goddam Fooler horse to that soap factory.

It was the twenty-eighth day of June and I was telling Wrangler, "Here we've come down here and spent a hell of a long winter makin' the best gather on this wild stock anybody ever made. We've made Jim Ed a lot richer, and now look what he's doin' to us. If he don't send some cowboys on down here to help us move this stuff into headquarters, I'm just goin' to turn 'em all loose back in the hills."

Now Wrangler knew I wasn't going to do this, and I knew I wasn't. We had to have that bonus and that paycheck or there wouldn't be no Fourth of July as far as we were concerned. Just the same my nerves was cracking and popping like a stick of frozen wood in a hot fire.

Then three hands rode up. If seventeen angels from heaven had stopped by for supper and each one of them had donated a pot full of gold for the Fourth of July, I couldn't of been any happier to see them. All the same, Jim Ed had squeezed every damn hour of time out of us he could. The least little thing and I was going to quit this chicken outfit. And I meant it, just like I meant about Old Fooler and the soap.

Well, we got the horses in and packed the mules and gathered the stock and started moving the herd toward headquarters.

I told one of the hands, "It's a good thing you boys showed up when you did because me and old Wrangler just had one catch rope left between us, and we would have had one hell of a fight to see which one got to use it to hang himself with."

I was in charge of the herd, so I worked it so that we moved past Vince Moore's outfit too late for breakfast and too early for lunch. I didn't feel like discussing Old Fooler in front of the other cowboys. The herd moved slow because we had so many young calves that tired easy on us. We spent half the time carrying them on the swells of our saddles. Two and a half days later I could see the big gate into headquarters. A horseback rider was setting there waiting.

I rode over by Wrangler and said, "Now take three guesses who that is up there waitin'."

Wrangler looked through them little pig eyes of his, humped his shoulders, and kind of scrooched his rump around in the saddle. "Why, I bet it's Santie Claus," he said, "just sittin' out there waitin' to pay us our bonus."

"That's right," I said. "Jim Ed Santie Claus Love."

Jim Ed reined back from the gate a ways, and I could see his hand moving up and down as he counted the cows and horses coming through. Now I had already made a bet with myself about what his first words would be. I was right.

"Hello, boys. Have a good winter?" And then, "Where's my bay horse?"

I didn't answer right away. I didn't want the other hands to hear. I told him we'd had a fine pleasant winter. No trouble a tall. The horses was broke out nice and gentle and we had made a good gather on the wild stuff.

"Where's my bay?" he asked again.

I told him about how we had only lost one head of stock and the lightning did that.

"Seems to me," he said, "that roan horse is scarred up somewhat worse than he was last fall."

"Oh, we had a little trouble with him," I said. "He's the sorriest son of a bitch I ever saw in my life. He ain't fit for nothin'—can't run, and won't work a rope," I lied.

"Can he buck?" Jim Ed asked. But before I could answer that question he hit me with another. "Where's my bay horse?" It was like an obsession, as they say.

I couldn't dodge it any longer. So I told him. He didn't say a word, but one of the other hands heard and yelled ahead to the others. They were all laughing. Even the cows was laughing. I could swear every damn one of them had a big grin on its face, baby calves, bulls, steers, and all.

Well, Jim Ed had crowded me just as far as he was going to. Just one more little thing and I was through.

We got on into headquarters, and just as nice as pie Jim Ed says, "Go get cleaned up. I know you boys will be wanting to head for town and the Fourth of July celebration."

Wrangler snorted through his flat nose.

Jim Ed went on: "Soon as you're all cleaned up come over to the house and I'll pay you off. You boys are going to need a little money over the Fourth."

The way he said it he made it sound like he was doing us the biggest favor on earth. We got all shaved and cleaned up slick as a judge on election day. Then we went over to see his highness.

"Come in, boys," he shouted. "Come on in here and set down. Amantha," he yelled out into the kitchen, "bring us that bottle of whiskey out of the cupboard."

Mrs. Amantha Love came in speaking to us like she wished to hell we would get out of her house and not track it up. I kept looking down at my boots to see if I had left any cow dung on them.

Jim Ed poured us a nice stiff drink. We downed her, then he let us have it. He picked up the money and said, "Now, boys, in all I owe you a five-hundred-dollar bonus. Five dollars a head for every one you gathered. Right?"

"That's right," I said. "What about the calves that was born this spring?"

Old Wrangler wiggled around on the edge of his chair trying to get his a bowlegs on the floor.

"Well, now, that wasn't part of our deal."

"We gathered them," I said. "They was right there in their mother's bellies when we penned them."

"It ain't quite the same thing," said Jim Ed. "There wasn't no trouble a tall to them calves. They just went along for the ride and there wasn't a damn thing they could do about it."

Well, I thought, *there went an extra hundred or so dollars.* Now where was the next cut coming from?

"I figured that bay horse was the best horse in the bunch," Jim Ed said. "He was worth at least sixty dollars." So, then and there Jim Ed counted sixty dollars out of our pile.

"That's it!" I said. "That does it! I quit! You can take the JL and shove it all the way back to that sorry Andrews, Texas, ranch you're always braggin' about owning. What about you, Wrangler?" I gathered up our money.

"Whatever suits you," he said, "just tickles me plumb to death."

Just as we hit the door, Jim Ed said, "Wait a minute, boys. I am goin' to give you that good Old Fooler horse in the place of that sixty dollars."

Well, I was so damn mad I was halfway to the bunkhouse before this soaked in on me. At least I would have the pleasure of getting even with that outlawed son of a bitch.

We threw our bedrolls and war bags in the old pickup. Then we loaded Old Fooler and jumped in. The goddam battery was dead! We had to push to beat hell to get it going downhill before it would start.

Jim Ed was standing on the porch waving and grinning like a cat eating a whole pile of it. He had a look on his face like he knew something we didn't.

I gave that old pickup all the gas she could take, and we went barreling out of there headed for Hi Lo, New Mexico. I wanted to get as far away from Jim Ed Love and the JL just as fast as I could. I knew Wrangler felt exactly the same.

TEN

Wrangler humped up over that steering wheel, frowning fierce over the top of it like he was fixing to pull the trigger on something or other. He sat on the edge of the seat so his crooked legs could reach the gas pedal. His little pot gut lay out in his lap.

"Wrangler," I said, "have you ever seen anything like that Jim Ed?"

Wrangler grunted.

"I cannot think of one single goddam thing in his favor," I went on.

Wrangler grunted.

"He is without a doubt the lowest-life son of a bitch in the world."

Wrangler grunted and stepped on the gas. The old pickup jerked and sputtered. Then she took hold and we really started to put ground between us and the JL.

About eight or ten miles off I could see the little Mexican village of Sano. It stuck right up out of the ground like a bunch of little square mud mountains. The adobe houses looked kind of lonesome and dried out from where we was.

I knew my good friend Telio Cruz ran one of those places just made to cure the thirst of dry-throated cowboys.

"Faster," I said to Wrangler.

"That's all she'll do," he said.

Sano crept closer, and I could see the rocky foothills beyond where in the old days a bunch of gold mines had operated. And on past that about a hundred miles I could see a long blue stretch of mountains. I figured that me and Wrangler could find an outfit over there that would appreciate a couple of dumb cowboys like us. Maybe we could get a half-decent job over there. Anyway, as soon as the Fourth of July was over we would sure as hell find out.

"God a'mighty, Wrangler, I'm goin' to die of thirst before we get to Telio's. Can't you speed this cockeyed heap up? If I didn't hate to walk so bad, I would just bail out of here and save time."

"If you're in such a big hurry," said Wrangler, "why don't you ride Old Fooler?"

I said, "I had just as soon have my head tied up in a sack full of feverish rattlesnakes! But even that would be better than dying of thirst."

Well sir, it seemed like forever but we finally got there. I spotted old Telio looking through a dirty window to see who was driving up. Wrangler pulled the pickup on around past the one gas pump and let her coast to a stop. The brakes needed adjusting or something, so he didn't have much choice.

Telio met us at the door, grinning out of that big fat face of his and smoothing his long black hair. When Telio smiled it was like a whorehouse chandelier. He must of had fifty teeth on the top side alone. Now, Telio ain't what you would call stupid. He could see that we was all cleaned up and he knew that meant we was going to the Fourth of July in Hi Lo. It also meant we had a pocket full of back pay.

"Come in, friends," he said, smiling like a million watts. "Long time no see. Welcome home. The first drink is on Telio."

While he was pouring her out I smelled that bar like a bird dog smells a covey of quail. It smelled like as much beer, wine, and some little whiskey had been spilled as had ever been drunk. It made my eyes sort of glaze over. Wrangler was stretching up as high as he could, trying to get his elbows comfortable on the bar. For a minute I thought he was going to jump right on over and help himself.

"How about a double shot to start with?" asked Telio.

"That's mighty nice of you, Telio," I said, knowing how little business he had.

"How did you boys winter?"

"Well, I reckon we wintered mighty fine," I said, not wanting to spoil the mood of things.

"How's Jim Ed?" he asked.

Me and Wrangler didn't answer but just threw our heads back and downed that double shot. Well, it burned somewhat going down and settled in my belly like a hot rock in a cold pond. My eyes smarted, and the naked girl on the beer calendar hanging behind the bar kind of blurred. Then things straightened up and got better.

"Give us another one," I said.

Down she went like a bolt off a tall windmill.

"Give that old boy over there a drink," Wrangler said, pointing to an old white-headed wino sitting in one of the high-backed booths across the room.

"Yeah, and another all around—only this time make it water on the side," I said.

The old man got up and walked over. He had a big hump on his back and his eyes was just oozing Dago red.

"He don't drink nothing but wine," said Telio.

"Give him all he wants," I said.

The old man smiled at us and without a word downed the whole glass. Then, polite-like, he nodded about five times, saying, "Gracias, señors, gracias."

Well sir, things got better all the time. I got to telling Telio what a great horse that was out there in the pickup, and he let me rave on for a while.

Then he went out and looked at him and said, "Shorty Wilson over at Hi Lo buys outlaws like that for fifteen dollars apiece."

This kind of set me back on my hunkers, but I asked, "What does he do with them?"

"He sells them to the dog food company up in Colorado."

"That's it!" I yelled. "Wrangler, did you hear that! That's a whole lot better than soap. I am goin' to sell him to them dog food people and buy the first can made out of him and feed that son of a bitch to the mangiest old cur of a hound dog I can find."

This made me feel so good that I sang out, "Give everybody in the house another drink."

Now somehow or other you can start a party in one of these Mexican bars with nobody around but the bartender, and pretty soon everybody in town is there. We now had six people in tow. Five Mexican-Americans and an Apache Indian, also a gringo salesman we didn't count.

Everybody kind of slipped up to the bar, and the first thing you know Telio was washing glasses just as fast as he could fill them up, and there was wine and beer running all over the cracks in the bar. Telio would take a quick swipe at it and grab up a bunch of empty glasses. Before he could get that bunch clean, we was hollering for a refill. Pretty soon he joined in by taking a drink now and then himself. Then he threw the bar towel on the floor and just left the same glasses out on the bar top. He was short on water anyhow, seeing as how it took so much for me and Wrangler to wash down his cheap whiskey.

Now, I'm telling you this place really filled up fast from there on in. I never saw so many amigos in all my life. And that's what they called us—shaking hands about every two or three seconds until I felt like my arm was going to fall right off. The old wino had gone over and fell asleep in one of the booths. Every once in a while he would raise his head, mumble something, and go right back to sleep.

Then this long tall old gringo with more whiskers than a porcupine has quills got me off to himself and started telling me about his gold mine.

He said, "Looky here." And sure enough, there in a little bottle was a half-dozen nuggets of gold about the size of a shriveled-up piñon nut. "I know where there is a vein of this ten feet wide," he said. "It assays eight hundred dollars to the ton in gold and one hundred and ninety dollars in silver."

"Well, I'll be damned," I said, trying to add this up in my mind. I didn't have any luck—just too many zeros at one time.

He looked at me out of little bitty watery blue eyes and pulled his greasy hat loose from around his ears and started bearing down on me.

"Them old-timers didn't have any modern machinery, and when they got to a vein like this they would all go crazy anyway. I know personally of twenty-five men killed over this very vein of gold. I am the only one left that knows about it."

"Well, I'll be damned," I said.

"All I need to bring out ten tons a day is some good powder, drill steel, and enough money to hire two good miners for a week. And of course some grub and hay for the burros. Do you realize how much profit a day that would be at ten tons?"

"Well—" I started to answer.

"Well," he interrupted, getting kind of excited-like, "let's figure it at only five tons. Let's be conservative. 'Course a vein that wide," he said, "you can really break a lot of rock. Figure it up," he insisted, looking me in the eye and breathing like a sheepherder at a beauty contest.

"It's a whole lot," I said, trying not to appear ignorant. "How much money would it take?"

"A hundred dollars," he said, "and half the profit's yours."

I got that hundred dollars out so fast you would have thought it was a tarantula in my pocket instead of cash.

"Here," I said, "write me General Delivery in Santa Fe, New Mexico. Make out the checks to Dusty Jones."

Well sir, that old prospector—name was Adams—felt so good about that grubstake that he ordered everybody in the house a drink of pure whiskey and paid for it out of the hundred.

Now the place was getting fuller. So was me and Wrangler. He had finally give up trying to get his elbows on the bar and instead was setting right up on top with his thick arms in the air telling a big lie to a bunch of drunk amigos. It was plain to see that he had got past the grunt and one-sentence stage.

All of a sudden, right out of nowhere—you might say right out of the clean, pure, fresh mountain air—a guitar and fiddle appeared. Two Spanish fellers with kindness in their hearts was going to furnish the music. It was the best I ever heard. The music got faster and louder. I never did know what they were playing. All I know is it was the best I ever heard.

Every once in a while Wrangler would throw his hands in the air and open his mouth and howl like a lobo with a belly full of sheep. Old Telio would pull his mouth around that head full of teeth and do a fancy jig behind the bar. Everybody was laughing, hollering, raising hell, and having a real good time. There was just one thing missing. A woman!

I was staring hard at the naked gal on the beer calendar, thinking that I would give all my interest in that gold mine (getting my pardner's agreement, of course) to have her for just one whole night. Then I got to thinking that I was bragging to myself a little maybe. I decided I would settle for a ten minutes.

Then Wrangler let out a yell like a young bull in a pasture full of two-year-old heifers. He jumped off that bar top and was running before his feet hit the floor. There it was, standing inside the door. A woman! Now, she didn't have no teeth and her nose swung down almost to her chin. Her hair wasn't black and it wasn't gray either. It was sort of in between. She was kind of wide and drooped in the hunkers like a hen laying an oversized egg, but the main thing is, she was a woman!

Wrangler gathered her up and got her over to the bar so fast it looked a little greedy on his part. Telio introduced her as Sophia and said she was the *seester* of the old wino sleeping over in the booth.

"A fine girl," he said.

We started buying her drinks just as fast as she could get them down. Sophia might not have been much for looks, but she sure could apply herself to them drinks we bought her. She'd run her tongue out when she a set her glass down and lick her chin so's not to waste a drop. Pretty soon Wrangler had her out in the middle of the floor and they were doing a "Folsom Stomp." (Folsom is a little town in northern New Mexico where they don't do much dancing but a hell of a lot of stomping.)

Finally I just couldn't stand it any longer and I ran out and jerked her loose from Old Wrangler and she really bellied up to me.

Things got better all the time. Them two old boys played the prettiest music I ever heard in my life. Yes sir, the best I ever heard. The more we whirled around, the more beautiful Sophia looked. Why, I never saw such lovely eyes, as them town fellers would say. And that hair . . . it shined like a fresh-brushed mane of a slick sorrel mare. I decided that the girl on the calendar couldn't hold a candle to my Sophia. Now there was one place I was wrong, and that was this *my* business. As it turned out, Sophia was *ours*.

Old Wrangler waltzed in there and shot me out of the saddle as slick as axle grease. He waltzed right on around by the door and slipped outside. It was just getting dark. His timing was right on the money. I hobbled back up to the bar. Old Telio winked at me and threw his head back and laughed. "Shut up, you drunken bum," I said, "and give me another drink." I stared at the girl on the calendar and decided she wasn't so bad after all.

After a while Wrangler came in grinning like a jackass eating briars and proved his friendship right then and there. He snuck up beside me. I could tell he wanted to speak quiet-like. I bent my ear down and he said, "She's waitin' for you out in the pickup."

Now, I never was no hand at taking seconds on anything. Howsomever, this was no time to argue principles. I ducked my head and tore on out.

After a little spell me and Sophia decided we needed another drink. We moseyed back inside. Hardly nobody paid any attention to us. Some of them was asleep at the bar. Two more was laying in the booths, and one was under a table in the back of the room. The rest was either struggling like hell to hold the bar up or was out in the middle of the floor jigging and hollering.

The party went on. A little priest came in and motioned for Telio to give him a glass of port wine.

"Wine, Father?" Telio asked. "Sure, Father, sure. It's on the house. Our dear Father is leaving us soon," he said to me with tears brimming out of his eyeballs and leaking down on the bar top. "After all these years," he said, "they are taking him away from us."

"Well, I'll be damned," I said. "When you leaving, Reverend?"

"Father!" Telio yelled at me.

"Father," I said, trying not to show my ignorance.

"The day after tomorrow," the Father said, shaking his head sadly.

"How come?" I asked. "How come they are doin' this thing to you?"

"I have been called elsewhere, my son," he said, gritting his teeth and bucking up. "My duty has called and I must answer."

"Not enough money in this parish," Telio said. "Not enough people. No funds to fix the church."

"I must go tomorrow and gather the Santos from our blessed little church on the hill," the Father said.

"Have another drink," I said.

He did. "Thank you, my son," he said.

"Well, if there is anything we can do to help, just call on us," I told him, feeling downright religious.

"There might be," he said. "You could help me move the bell."

"The bell!" yelled Telio. "That's my bell. Father, I want that bell back. You know I am a good Catholic," he went on, "and I pray to the saints. I go to mass. I am steady at confession but I will not let them take the bell. It is bad enough that we lose you, Father," Telio said, pouring another glass of port. "A good priest like you is hard to find. But the bell! I traded three sheep, a goat, and a suckling pig for it."

"Do not anguish yourself, my son," said the Father, shaking his empty glass under Telio's weeping eyes. "We will return your bell."

Telio filled his glass.

It came a time when I could not stand to hear Telio yap about his bell any longer. "Let's go get the goddam bell," I said.

"I cannot leave the bar," said Telio. "Look." He waved a fat arm around.

"I can see that," I said. "Well, me and Wrangler will go with the priest and get your bell."

"You will have my undying blessing to follow you across the earth," said Telio.

I said, "Well, I sure appreciate that. Come on, Father," I said, "let's get goin'."

"Yes, my son, let's do. We must not keep from Telio what is his any longer."

It seems we was having quite a time keeping Wrangler from what was ours. He was out in the pickup again with Sophia.

I got a bottle from Telio, telling him the drinks were on us till we got back. Me and the Father strolled out of there and climbed in the pickup with Wrangler and Sophia. It was a little crowded, but we all kind of scrounged up together and made room. Old Fooler was snorting and eyeballing around in the back end. For a little while I had forgotten about him and Jim Ed. It had been a good feeling.

I drove off up toward the little run-down church on the hill. Wrangler was snuggling up to Sophia, telling her what a great woman she was. Me and the Father was taking a little slug out of the bottle to keep from hearing all them gooey words Wrangler was using.

We pulled up in front of the church. There the bell was, hanging up there in the steeple. The moonlight was shining so bright, for a minute I thought the sun was coming up.

We all crawled out and took a little slug out of the bottle so we wouldn't catch cold. I let ol' Fooler out of the truck and walked him around about three minutes before reloading him.

"How we goin' to get up there?" I asked.

"Well, my son," the Father said, "that does pose a problem."

Wrangler had one of his rare ideas then. He pointed to an elm tree that was growing beside the church and hung out over it.

"You are showing signs of intelligence again, Wrangler," I said and commenced to climb the tree. I made it all right for a while and crawled out on a limb like a big-ass bird.

Every time I would bend over to reach for the bell the limb would get to swaying and I would damn near fall off. I could hear my three friends down below cheering me on and passing the bottle back and forth. It was just what I needed to hear. I leaned way on out and reached for the bell. The limb broke. I fell. I kept falling for a long time, it seemed like to me. When I kind of came to, I thought I had died and was at my funeral. Then I saw a streak of light, and a match flared.

There I was setting right smack in the middle aisle of the church and there was the bell where it had come through the roof with me.

The bell had gone right on through the floor. I got up slow, wondering if I had busted my leg again. It felt all right.

I said, "Wrangler, strike another match."

He did. It took all of us to get that bell up out of the floor, ringing to beat hell all the while.

I said, "I'm sure sorry, Father, about tearing up your church."

"It does not matter, my son," he said. "It will go back to dust now just as you and I." He had me kind of rattled for a minute. Then he said, "It is a courageous thing you have done this night. I am sure Telio's prayers will follow you forever."

That sounded mighty good to me, and also it meant that Fooler horse might not be going to kill me after all, if I was going to be around that long.

ELEVEN

Something woke me up. Whatever it was, it was prizing my jaws apart. I sat up in my bedroll and saw my prospecting pardner, Adams.

"You got my teeth?" he asked.

"Hell, no!" I yelled. "I've had these ever since I was a kid."

"I lost my teeth," he mumbled through his beard. He got up and stared around kind of helpless-like.

I said: "Why don't you go find Sophia? She's a smooth mouth. Maybe she's usin' them."

"I lost 'em," he said, and stumbled off down the road toward Sophia's place. I was sure hoping he'd find them so he would get on up in the mountains and dig for our gold.

Wrangler raised up in his bedroll, pushing his tangled hair out of his eyes. I don't think it made any difference about his hair. His eyes was so swelled up and red that he couldn't see anyway. They looked like two burnt holes in a saddle blanket.

"Good morning, glory," I said.

Wrangler was not on one of his talking spells. He didn't even grunt.

Then I saw the bell hanging on the pickup and Old Fooler tied around to the side with an empty oat bucket by him. I didn't remember hanging the bell, and I didn't remember letting Old Fooler out of the pickup.

Old Fooler nickered and looked back over his shoulder.

I could tell he wanted a drink. I got dressed and led him across the street to a horse trough. I washed my face and combed my hair while Old Fooler drank. The sun was just coming up and the roosters was all through crowing.

Then I heard the door to the bar slam and here came Telio. He had not bothered to comb his hair or even push it out of his eyes. He looked like a bareheaded hermit in a cyclone.

"Come on over to my house and I will get you some breakfast," he said.

"Naw," I said. "We'll drive on over to Hine's Corner. It's on Highway 202 and we can whip right on into Hi Lo from there. We can get breakfast there and maybe a drink."

I knew that according to New Mexico law the bars was not supposed to open till nine o'clock. It was about six now.

Telio said, "Come on over, I will get you a drink. There is no law here," he added, reading my mind.

Wrangler had his head plumb under water. I thought for a minute he was trying to drown himself. Then he came up for air. We stumbled over to Telio's and got us a drink. It was as hard to get down as a bucket full of mud, and when it hit bottom I was sure it would bounce.

I didn't think Old Wrangler could look any worse than he did just natural, but after swallowing his shot he made a face that would have caused his own mother to hang herself. I doubt if he had a mother anyway. I don't think he was born at all. I'm pretty sure Wrangler just hatched out from under some old bear droppings.

By the time we had a couple more, things were beginning to look up. I said, "Wrangler, you ready to pull out to Hine's Corner and get some grub in our bellies?"

"Whatever suits you just tickles me plumb to death," he said.

We did up our bedrolls and loaded Old Fooler back in the

pickup. Then I noticed the bell again. I also noticed where my hide was peeled in several places.

I yelled at Telio, "Come out here and get your bell!"

"It ain't mine," he yelled back. "It's yours. You gave me twenty-five dollars for it last night."

"Well, I'll be damned," I said. I decided I had better tie something around that bell to keep it from ringing. Old Fooler must have had a fit when we drove down from the church last night. Telio brought me a gunnysack and I tied it around the belt.

We crawled in the pickup and took off. The clapper swung back and forth but it didn't make much noise, which was a damn good thing, the way my head was hollowed out from the sporting activities of the past night.

It wasn't long until we hit the pavement. It was mighty nice riding and the first time we had been out of the sand, timber, and rocks for a long time. Before we hardly knew it, there was Hine's Corner. It was a big restaurant and bar as well as a curio store selling Indian trinkets to the tourists. Highway 27 crossed with Highway 202 and Hine's Corner joined them both. It was a welcome sight.

We crawled out of that old pickup and walked into the restaurant part. It was still too early for the bar to be open.

Well sir, another sight to make a man sling his head and wring his tail like a bronc on the first saddling stood right there behind the counter—a little old brown-haired, blue-eyed gal built like a registered quarter horse. She smiled at us as we came in.

"Sit down, boys, and make yourselves at home," she said. She handed us a menu. It was a low counter, and Wrangler didn't have no trouble at all getting his elbows on it. He wasn't reading the menu but was aiming out over the top of it at this gal. I don't think he can read anyway.

I took over for both of us, seeing as how he was so "enamored," as the town fellers say. "Give us three eggs apiece, a stack of hotcakes, a big chunk of ham, and about a half a gallon of coffee," I said.

"How do you want your eggs?" this toothsome thing asked.

"Just cooked," I said.

Well now, it came as sort of a shock to look up and see another one just as pert stick her head out of the kitchen stall and take the order. She looked out at us and she smiled too. Old Wrangler just spun around on the counter stool and started pawing the floor. It looked for a minute like he was going to run back there and ear her down right on the cookstove.

It was a right good breakfast. One of the best I ever had. Wrangler took out a five-dollar bill and went back to tip the cook. He stayed quite a while, even after three or four truck drivers had stopped to order breakfast. I just kept drinking coffee and eyeballing the waitress.

Come to find out these two gals had leased this place about three months back. The cook was named Kate and the waitress was Mary.

It surprised me to hear this because I had once worked a team of mules by the same names. Of course, I didn't mention this to the girls.

Mary looked at me out of those blue eyes and said, "You boys heading for the rodeo at Hi Lo?"

"Yeah," I said. "Why don't you and Kate come along?"

"Sure wish we could," she said, and slung her head kind of sad-like.

Time flies, and it wasn't long till Mary opened the bar. Another waitress stopped in and took her place in the kitchen. I told Wrangler to come on in the bar and we would have a bottle of beer to wash our breakfast down.

He didn't much like leaving Kate. I reckon, though, that salty ham had made him thirsty.

"It must have been a bigger breakfast than we thought," I said to Wrangler. "We have already had six bottles of beer apiece and I'm still thirsty."

"Give us anothern," he said, peering around the bar, trying to see into the kitchen.

"Have a drink, Mary," I said.

"Can't now, boys. Against my rules. Too early. Now, if you boys were to be around here about nine tonight when Kate closes the restaurant . . ."

"It's a long time till nine," I said.

Wrangler said, "You know something?"

"What?" I asked.

"Time flies," he said.

"You're right," I said. And it did.

About the middle of the afternoon a man and woman pulled up out front in a New Jersey car. They had two kids with them, a boy about six and a little yellow-headed girl a year or two older.

They fooled around out in the curios for a little while and then moseyed into the bar. They sat down and ordered a coke apiece for the kids and a bottle of beer for themselves.

"Sure hot outside," the woman said.

"Oh, it's not bad," Mary said, "for this time of year."

"Oh," she said, trying to get her hunkers to fit on the bar stool all at one time. The old boy glanced through his glasses at me like he knew me. He sat there pushing his long-billed canvas cap back and forth on his head and rubbing his belly, which was bigger than Wrangler's. His wife seemed worried about her looks and kept staring at herself in the back mirror, twisting her head like a one-eyed hound at a treed coon.

The little girl walked over to us and said, "Are you cowboys?"

"Well," I told her, "I ain't yet. But if I keep practicin' and get rid of that horse out there in the pickup I might make it someday."

"You look like cowboys to me," she said, turning around to stare out the window at Old Fooler.

"What a beautiful horse," her mother said.

"Yes, lady," I said, "that horse is just like a patch of locoweed."

"What in the world is that?" she said, squinting out over her overfed cheeks.

"It's a purty little green weed that once in a while comes up in the springtime before anything else."

"What's so bad about that?" she asked.

"There ain't nothin' bad about its purty color," I went on. "It's just that after a long winter, the stock is starvin' for somethin' green. Well, naturally they tie into this locoweed and that's what's bad."

"Why?"

I said, "It gives them the blind staggers, headaches, bellyaches, the shaky trembles, and the scared boogers. Besides that," I said, "it drives them plumb slap dab crazy."

"Goodness!" she said.

"Well, lady," I told her, "that is exactly the effect that beautiful horse out there has on mankind. That is why I have quit my job and turned my pardner here to strong drink."

She looked out the window with new interest.

The little boy was looking up at me with his ears flopping in the wind. "Where's your gun?" he said, looking right hurt because I didn't jerk it out and shoot a hole in the wall.

"I ain't got no gun, son," I said. "My pardner here has one in his war bag. But he's a little loco hisself, and we can't take any chances on him."

Wrangler snorted through his busted nose and took a half bottle of beer down his gullet with one swallow. The kid promptly lost interest in me and tied into old Wrangler, but he couldn't get him to talk. Pretty soon he said, "Aw, you ain't cowboys anyway. Bat Masterson would run you out of town in five minutes."

I said, "Son, if he will ride Old Fooler for five minutes first, I will be glad to take him on in a gun battle and spot him seven seconds' head start on the draw."

"Aw-ww," he said, and walked out into the curio and bought himself a Roy Rogers, the King of the Cowboys, comic book. He kept reading this out loud until his pa said, "Sonny, go on out to the car and read."

This boy looked at me and Wrangler again and said, "Roy Rogers would shoot you so full of holes so quick you wouldn't even have time to turn around."

I said, "Give that boy a coke, Mary, before he gets us bums killed."

Wrangler said, as if I'd included him in the coke business, "I want a beer."

I got up and played the jukebox. While I was standing there the little girl walked over and said, sweet-like, "I don't care what Ronny thinks; I believe you're real cowboys. You're just being modest. I bet you can outdraw anybody."

"That's right, honey," I said, patting her on the head. "I am the best hand in the world at drawin' the rough string. Ever' outfit I go to work for turns 'em over to me."

Ma and Pa got up and left. They had to drag little Ronny with them. He was practicing his fast draw and cocking his thumb back, filling me and old phony Wrangler plumb full of holes like a real cowboy would have done.

That jukebox was making my feet itch. I jumped up and did a fast jig. Old Wrangler clapped his hands and yelled like an opera singer with her bloomers on fire. Things were getting better all the time.

I went out and tied Old Fooler to the side of the pickup and fed him some oats. After while I took him around in the back of the store to water him, and saw a little catch pen. So I put him in there and he nibbled around on some weeds and old hay.

I said to him, "Eat while you can, you son of a bitch. It won't be long till the hungry dogs will be eatin' *you*."

He looked up at me kinda funny-like. I shot him with my finger like little Ronny and went back to the bar, feeling good.

Now nine o'clock came and things got even better. Kate closed up the restaurant and came in and sat down between me and Wrangler and ordered a screwdriver—whatever the hell that is. She had two more before old Wrangler decided it was moving time. He jerked her off that stool, and you talk about dancing! Well sir, those two really put on a show. Of all the jumping and hollering and fancy stepping, that was it. I got Mary to take a few shots with me and we joined them out in the middle of the floor. You talk about a couple of good sports, we had them. As time moved on, the dancing slowed down, and the first thing I knew we was stopped—not saying nothing, just holding one another like a couple of school-kids on a midnight hayride. It was a right nice place to be.

We all went into the back rooms where the girls lived. We took us along some bottles and the girls pushed a button on one of them fancy Victrolas and the party was started. These gals wanted to know all about me and Wrangler, but all I could think to tell them about myself was to cuss Jim Ed Love and Old Fooler. They said they knew Jim Ed and thought he was a nice feller. I didn't answer that because I knew what a hand-shaking, ass-kissing, goody-goody he could be when he was out and about among the citizens. It wouldn't have done me or them any good either if I had told them what a slave-driving, dollar-hoarding old son of a bitch he really was.

But when it came to Old Fooler, I wouldn't back down, and then finally Wrangler said something that made me turn back to the party.

"Dusty," he said, holding Kate in his lap and feeding her whiskey out of the bottle, "you keep goin' on about what you are goin' to do with that horse when we get into Hi Lo. I'll bet you a month's wages that when the Good Lord sends you to hell you will be ridin' Old Fooler, and he will be buckin' to beat sixty."

"There is a number of ways to look at that," I said, "but I am going to take your bet." With that I gathered Mary up and said, "Honey, it's motel time. What do you say?"

Here's what she said: "I like you, honey, and whatever suits you just tickles me plumb to death."

For a minute I was about half jealous, figgering she had been out with my pardner, even though we did share and share alike. Then I laughed out loud—for old Wrangler was saying the same thing to Kate.

It was a short night.

TWELVE

It was around noon before anybody tried to get up at Hine's Corner. The first thing I heard was old Wrangler stirring around hunting a drink of water. It took some doing, but we all made it in for breakfast. Now, the more of that water I drank, the more I felt like I did the night before. It wasn't long till we decided we needed a cold beer to sober up on. Then after that we took another to get to feeling better. Then one more to keep the last one from fizzling out. And so it went.

By about mid-afternoon I asked a mighty big question. "Girls," I said, "it is too late to open this business up now. Why don't we all just crawl in that old pickup and lope on over to Hi Lo for the Fourth?"

At first the girls didn't think that would be a good idea, seeing as how they were just getting started in a new business, but after about two more beers and a screwdriver apiece the mood changed.

Mary said, "Hi Lo is the best town in the United States. We haven't been to a good rodeo in three years. Dusty, darling," she went on, "I don't think you have had a better idea since you were a baby boy."

It didn't take us very long to load Old Fooler and get a case of beer and two fifths of whiskey for medicine. It was somewhat crowded in the front of that pickup, but a man that would gripe about that would gripe about having to stand up on a train headed straight for heaven.

The girls wanted to know about the bell, and I said we were delivering it to a church in Hi Lo.

Then we got to singing. Now Wrangler sometimes gets it into his head that he has got quite a voice. Well, he has. It makes up for good with loud. It was not so much that we were singing different songs that made it sound so wild, but that Goddam Fooler had to join in and nicker to beat hell once in a while. It kind of threw the whole thing off key because he was even louder than Wrangler.

Along in the shank of the afternoon we could see Hi Lo shooting up out in the middle of a big country full of green grama grass. I spotted a clump of brush just off the road at about the same time.

"Let's stop here and have a picnic," I said.

Wrangler said, "We ain't got no sandwiches."

I said, "There is lots of things you can do on a picnic besides eat."

So we all bailed out and took our bedrolls to have something to set on and started opening up them beer cans and taking a slug now and then out of the fifths.

Well, the first thing I knew it was dark and we had to gather up a little wood and build a fire. It was right pleasant to set around that fire and tell lies and sing songs and snuggle up to that good-looking Mary woman.

When the fire went out I was too drunk to gather any more wood, and Wrangler and Kate had drug their bedroll off a ways to be by themselves. I didn't want to bother them. Mary said she didn't know much about what who was doing what and felt like we ought to retire for the evening. I sided right in with this line of thinking.

It was another short night.

About thirty minutes before daylight, I rared right straight up in bed. "God a'mighty," I said, "today is the Fourth of July! Get up!" Then I went to jumping into my clothes. It took some more yelling and a little bedroll-shaking before I could get anybody else to open their eyes. They were all acting drunk-like.

Mary sat up and said, "We haven't been in bed over ten minutes. I'm still tanked."

"It don't matter," I said. "You will have time to sober up before the rodeo."

It was darker than an apple cellar, and Wrangler was having a hell of a time getting Kate to stir. We finally got loaded in the pickup and took off in a big hurry.

I didn't have my eyes open very good, and since Wrangler wouldn't drive I was having a hard time herding the pickup down the middle of the road. I just aimed right down the white line and tried to keep her there. It was getting daylight, and we weren't very far from Hi Lo.

About that time Kate's eyes flew wide and she screamed, "I saw a black cat run across the road!"

Wrangler grunted and said, "Don't let it worry you, honey; he wasn't all black."

"Yes, he was," Kate said.

"Naw," Wrangler said, "he had a white butthole."

This seemed to satisfy Kate, and all of them but me went back to sleep. Well, the sun came up and I could see the dust boiling up off the ranch roads all around Hi Lo where the people was coming in pickups and wagons for the Fourth of July.

I had to drive slow considering my condition, and the sun was up pretty high when I pulled into Hi Lo.

Now I had forgotten about the bell. Just as we started down the main street we hit a bump and it began to ring like every church in the world was right here in Hi Lo. I reckon the clapper had flopped back and forth until it had worn through the gunnysack. Old Fooler began to buck and kick, and I mean kick. The pickup was rocking to beat hell, and I thought he was going to turn it over. People was stopping and staring like a bull at a bastard calf. It made me nervous.

I whipped off into a little vacant lot between two buildings, and by the time I had pumped those sorry brakes enough to get them to take hold I had run plumb across the lot out onto another street. There wasn't near so many people here, so I brought her to a stop.

Old Fooler was still trying to kick the pickup to smithereens, and every time he let fly the bell would ring.

I looked around. My pardner and the two women were damn sure awake now. I said, "Let's get to hell out of here before the law arrives."

Then I noticed something that made my eyes smart something terrible. We had left the picnic grounds in such a hurry and everybody kind of numb from all that drinking that the girls hadn't put on all their clothes.

Wrangler was awake enough now to know he had a half-dressed woman in his lap. Just then who came walking over toward the pickup but Shorty Wilson, the horse buyer.

I jumped out, telling my friends to stay put and I would think of something. Wrangler jerked a bottle out of the glove compartment and they all took a drink. I ran out to meet old Shorty with my hand outstretched. When I got ahold of him I shook hands like he had just saved me from cannibals. Every time he would try to break loose and get over close to the pickup I would shake some more and say, "It sure is good to see you, Shorty. By God, I really miss my old friends. How's the horse business, Shorty? How's the old lady and the kids? Shorty, my friend, come with me, I want to buy you a drink."

He got kind of wild-eyed and tried to break away. "I want to say hello to Wrangler," he said.

"Aw, he's drunk," I said, "and needs his sleep bad." I drug him off toward the Wild Cat Saloon with him looking back over his shoulder every whipstitch. Old Fooler was still bucking and kicking and falling down.

"What'll you take for the outlawed son of a bitch?" he asked.

"We'll talk trade later. I just can't wait another minute to get me a drink."

It wasn't easy, but I finally got him over to the Wild Cat. We had a couple of fast ones and I told him to wait right here. I would be back after a while and have a visit.

I stumbled down the street trying to figure what to do. If we went back after the rest of their clothes it would be too late to get my entry fee in for the rodeo, much less have time for any breakfast. If we didn't eat, me and Wrangler was sure going to make fools out of ourselves at that rodeo. It was not a very pleasant thought.

I saw the Hot Biscuit Café across the street. Arlee Barton, the feller that ran it, was a friend of mine. I stumbled in, and Arlee ran over shaking hands and asking questions.

I said, "Arlee, we have been friends a long time. I want you to do me a favor and not ask no more questions. You see that last booth way back there in the corner? Well, cook up four orders of bacon and eggs with coffee all around and loan me two of them aprons like the waitress over there is wearing."

Arlee said, "What you want them aprons for?"

I said, "Don't ask me no questions, you son of a bitch; just get 'em for me like the good friend you are, old friend."

Arlee went back and got me two aprons from the kitchen. "This is all I have," he said.

Well, I hotfooted it back to the pickup. Old Fooler had calmed down some. Kate was taking the last swallow out of the bottle. I handed them the aprons and said, "Here, put these on."

The girls did and stepped out. Well sir, their fronts was covered up pretty good, but the glare from the backs was about blinding in the morning sunshine.

Now, as I have said before, there is times that old Wrangler shows a faint glimmering of intelligence. This was one of those rare occasions. He pulled off that big old hat of his and slapped it over Kate's rear end. I didn't say anything, but I took mine off and did the same for Mary. Now it looked like if we worked fast we could make it over to the Hot Biscuit without getting throwed in jail.

We marched along, stepping out like Old Fooler does when he's just throwed me straight up. People was stopping and staring all up and down the street. They weren't looking at the girls but was just wondering what in the hell two cowboys was doing with their hats off so early in the day. The sun was getting pretty hot too. It kind of gave me the staggers.

We got in and I could hear stools turning like rusty wagon wheels all along the counter. We came to a stop at the last booth where the waitress was just putting our grub out. I sure thought she was slow about it.

"Now, girls," I said, "I'm going to count three, then me and Wrangler will not waste any time. I want you to jump in them seats like a ground squirrel dodgin' a fox."

Off came the hats! Down went the fannies!

"We done 'er," Wrangler said.

We wore our hats all during breakfast. Arlee kept looking over at me. He acted like he never seen a girl in an apron before. I walked over and whispered in his ear, "Keep your big mouth shut, or I will stomp you right smack through the floor."

"Take it easy," he said. "Take it easy."

"I will," I said. I walked back over to the booth and finished my breakfast.

"Wrangler, I am goin' down and enter us in the rodeo. Then I'm goin' over to the mercantile and buy these girls some dresses. What color do you like?" I asked.

Kate said, "Blue. Any color, just so it's blue."

Mary said, "Red will just be fine, but hurry. There's a draft."

"What do you want me to enter you in, Wrangler?"

"Bareback bronc ridin', wild-cow milkin', and bull ridin'," he said.

"Don't you want in the calf ropin'?"

"Nawww," he said, "I ain't got no horse."

"That's right," I said. "I'm goin' to sell Old Fooler to Shorty Wilson." I stumbled out of there feeling some relief at just being away from them associates of mine, as the town fellers say.

I stopped an old boy on the street carrying an entry blank and asked, "Where do you sign up?"

He pointed across the street to a vacant store building. It was old L. C. Work furnishing the stock and taking the entry money.

"Howdy, Dusty, what in the hell you doin' in town? Don't you know you're gettin' too old and broke up to rodeo?"

"Yeah," I said, shaking hands with L. C. and Glen Frazier, one of his helpers. "But you know me, L. C., my middle name is ignorance."

I got Wrangler entered in the events he wanted. I signed up for the wild-cow milking and calf roping.

"Ain't you going to get in the saddle-bronc ridin'?" he asked, looking kind of puzzled.

"Hell, no!" I said. "There is an old bald-faced roan horse over in my pickup that has done nothin' but take me for a bronc ride for the last eight or nine months."

"Maybe you'd ought to sell him to me for a buckin' horse," L. C. said, only half joking.

"I would," I said, "but that would be too good a fate for him. I'm goin' to sell him to Shorty Wilson for dog meat."

I peeled out the money and paid off. I told the boys adios, and I would see them at one o'clock out at the arena. A bunch more young hands came in to sign up.

I went over to the mercantile and walked back to where a bunch of a dresses hung on a rack. A woman about fifty years old with a grin as big as Telio the bartender's came dogtrotting up and said, "What can I do for you?"

I said, "With no offense intended, lady, but if I was to tell you, you would just haul off and knock me in the head."

She kind of reared back on her heels, stuck her belly out, and folded her arms over it. "Would you like a dress? What size? What color?"

"I can't remember the size," I said, "but I want one red and one blue. Better make them pretty big," I said. "These are growed-up, fitted-out women."

She got them all wrapped up, not saying much, and I paid her off. Then I scooted back to the restaurant.

"What took you so long?" Wrangler wanted to know.

"Time flies," the girls said together.

Kate said, "This booth has got splinters."

I said, "Your troubles are over," and handed the package to Mary.

I asked Arlee if it would be all right to run the cook out of the kitchen a minute so our friends could get dressed without going outside to the two-holer. I stared him hard in the eye, and he nodded.

The girls got up. Off came our hats and we covered for them till they went through the swinging door into the kitchen. I sat down and swallowed a big bait of that pure clean, fresh café air.

"What did you enter yourself in?" Wrangler asked.

I told him.

He said, "Calf ropin'? I thought you said—"

"By God!" I said, "I forgot I didn't have no horse. Now I'll have to rope off Old Fooler. God a'mighty, isn't this goin' to be some Fourth of July?"

The girls came back out and I was damn sure glad they were drunk. If they had been sober they would have brought the meat cleaver out of the kitchen with them and split my head down the middle plumb to my goozle. The dresses was way too short, coming just to their knees. And when you talk about fitting around the middle, why they had to make three wraps to get them to stay on. They had tied a big bowknot in their belts and came prancing out of there like they was dressed to go to a wedding.

I said, "Let's go over to the Wild Cat. I have got to see Shorty Wilson and tell him I can't let him have Old Fooler till after the show."

I wanted to get them over there and buy them some more drinks.

It was a worrisome way to start the Fourth of July.

We stepped out on the street and heard a band playing. I could hear Old Fooler kicking again and that bell ringing. I hoped nobody would notice.

Here came the parade. First the school band, then horsebackers of all kinds, from the brushiest cowboys to the fattest, softest businessmen, kids on broken-down plow horses and some whey-bellied ranchers like Jim Ed on good-looking quarter horses.

Then there was the rodeo queen in a big paper-hung float, and I'm telling you there was some fancy cars and wagons following. It was a sight to see, but I couldn't afford to stand idle and watch it all.

I said, "Come on, folks, Shorty is waitin'." And we went in the Wild Cat and ordered a drink for the house.

The Fourth of July was on!

THIRTEEN

After the parade everybody started filing out toward the Hi Lo arena. On one side of the arena is a grandstand, and on the other side folks just park their cars right up against the fence and get out and set on the fenders. Under the grandstand is a hamburger and soda-pop booth. A half-mile racetrack runs around the arena. The bucking chutes face north with the holding corrals for the broncs, wild cows, and bulls just behind. The calf pen and chutes face east, and it's a good long run from one end to the other.

The cowboys get down to the rodeo grounds earlier than the spectators. When we drove up in the pickup there was horse trailers parked all over the place. Ropers and bulldoggers were brushing, saddling, and reining out their horses all around us. Some of them was standing around throwing loops over their rope cans or a bale of hay. The bronc riders was testing out the fit of their stirrups on association saddles, and the bareback riders were checking over spurs and riggin'. A lot of these boys had enough ability to go right on into professional rodeo. Most of them wouldn't, though, because of having to stay on the ranch or doing something else.

We unloaded Old Fooler and I saddled him up. The girls opened us a can of cold beer. Now, usually I don't like to drink before a show. But this time I was in such a shape that it didn't make a whole lot of difference one way or the other.

Old Coy Beasly rode over on his big brown roping quarter horse and asked what I was going to rope off of. I told him, "This here horse right here."

He looked at Old Fooler and said, "Well-put-together horse, but he looks like he has recently been in a wreck."

"He has," I said. "Several."

I hated to see old Coy show up. He was always beating me out of first money everywhere we went. Seems like he never beat a feller bad—maybe one, two-tenths of a second, but that was just as good as five minutes.

I got on Old Fooler, quivering all over, and rode him easy-like down to look at the calves. I had drawn Number Twelve—a big gray flop-eared brahma. I would really have to jerk him down hard if I was going to make any time on that big booger.

Several of the other contestants rode up looking for their calves. Finally I went off, trying to get up nerve enough to break Old Fooler out of a walk. I knew if I busted out of that roping box in a dead run before getting him warmed up there would be a whole lot more of a bronc ride than a calf roping. I rode over to where Wrangler was climbing up on the fence to look at his bronc.

"Which one did you draw?" I asked.

"That little black son of a bitch," he said. "They say he really turns it on."

"That's good," I said. "You wouldn't have no chance on a runaway."

The girls said they was going over in the grandstand and would see us after the show. It suited me because I couldn't get my thoughts on them anyhow, seeing how nervous I was about Old Fooler.

Well, the grandstand was beginning to fill up and the music was pouring out over the loudspeaker. Cars was lined up solid along the south fence. Cowboys and horses were everywhere, and the dust was beginning to powder around the arena.

Then the music stopped and Sy Wheeler, the announcer, began blowing in the mike, testing it out. He said, "All right, all you cowboys gather down at the east end of the arena and get ready for the grand entry."

We all lined up behind a couple of local boys carrying flags. One carried the U.S. flag and the other the State of New Mexico flag. All of a sudden the music started up and we all spurred out into the arena. We circled in a good lope behind the two flag-bearers. After about three times around the arena, we lined up and faced the grandstand. They played what Wrangler calls the Star-Spangled Bandanner, for a joke. We all took off our hats. When it was over we made one more circle and rode out of the arena.

Then Sy Wheeler started welcoming everybody to the annual Hi Lo Fourth of July celebration and hoped they enjoyed the show and had a good time. Then he introduced L. C. Work, who was furnishing the stock, and Bill and Angus Blair, the pickup men.

The show was on!

The bareback bronc riding led it off. . . .

"Grady Decker on the bucking horse Sundown comin' out of Chute Number One!"

The big bay ran a little ways, ducked his head, and threw poor old Grady on the second jump.

"Hard luck, cowboy. Give him a hand, folks; that's all the pay he's going to get."

Grady got up, dusting himself off, and stumbled back toward the bucking chutes, trying to get his hat back in place.

One after the other the broncs poured out. A little Mexican from Española kicked the mane out of one and looked like he had first money cinched.

Then I heard the announcer say, "Wrangler Lewis on Black Devil comin' out of Chute Number Three!"

I spurred over so I could watch. Well, it was good. That little black bastard came out with his head down, bucking the first jump out of the chute. Old Wrangler was setting way up on top of the gloved hand where he was holding onto the handle of the bareback riggin'. He had his spurs up high in that black's neck. The black went up and came down twisting. He never hit twice going in the same direction. It looked once like Wrangler was going off, but he righted himself and kept raking them spurs back and forth. I could see where he had loosened the last two snaps on his chaps so they would flap and make it look like he was spurring a lot harder. Lots of cowboys think this fools the judges, but it don't.

Well, the whistle blew to signal the end of his ride. Old Wrangler jumped off and landed on his feet. It sure was pretty. The crowd clapped to beat hell. I figured Wrangler had sewed up second money if the next and last rider didn't beat him.

The last rider was Sowbelly Jenkins. He must have been forty-five years old, an age when most bronc riders are either dead or crippled. Sowbelly was tough but he drew a runaway horse that bucked just enough so he couldn't get a reride and not enough to put him in the money. By God, things had started off all right.

Sy was calling the ropers and telling the next man he was up and the third man to get ready. I was way down the line. Well, the first boys was a little overanxious, and missed. Then Art Walker sailed out there and fit it on one before he hardly started.

Coy Beasly to me, "There goes the money."

But it didn't. Art's horse didn't keep the rope tight, and the calf got to circling on him and it took eighteen and six-tenths seconds to tie his calf. Well, there was a twenty-second catch and tie and another miss. Then an eighteen-two. Then a seventeen-eight and so on down the line.

The seventeen-eight was still first money when Coy Beasly rode in the chute. He came out of there fast after that calf. But he really had himself a runaway. The brown horse built to him and Coy reached out with his rope and fit it on, and he come off his horse running and wrapped that calf up in seventeen flat.

Sy Wheeler said, "That's the fastest time of the day, folks."

Well, here it was. I was next up. At least I knew what I had to beat. I reined Old Fooler out into the arena in front of the roping box. I want the world to know that my gut was sucking wind. There was just no telling what kind of ungodly stunt that Fooler horse would pull out here in front of all these people.

I rode him into the box and turned him around. He backed right up with his tail against the back end of that box, his head up, and his ears throwed forward. I could feel him quivering all over just a little. Then I knew that son of a bitch had been here before, too. I was beginning to wonder where he *hadn't* been.

I had my piggin' string in my mouth. I took a deep seat in the saddle and tucked the upper strand of my loop under my right arm, so it wouldn't drop down and hang under a stirrup. Then I took part of the loop in my right hand and gathered in that saddle horn. I looked out at the man working the calf chute and could see the rope barrier stretched tight across the roping box and the barrier man standing with a flag in his hand holding the pull-rope, waiting for my signal. Now, when the calf was turned loose and his head came to a line fifteen feet in front of the chute, the barrier man would jerk that rope away. If I broke the barrier before the proper time, I would be fined ten seconds' penalty, and no matter how fast I tied I would be out of the money.

There was no use waiting any longer. I nodded my head at the chute man. He jerked the gate open, and the calf came out running at full speed for the other end. I waited just that half-second so I wouldn't break the barrier, then leaned over on Old Fooler. God almighty! He tore out of there so hard I thought he was bucking at first. It took me a little longer than I wanted to be able to turn loose of that saddle horn. A calf roper has got plenty to think about anyway, besides whether his horse is going to buck and run off.

I brought that loop up and whirled her about three times and there was the calf, right where I wanted him. Old Fooler skinned up to him fast with his ears laid back. The calf headed off to the right just a little. That's where he made his mistake. I let that loop fly and it whipped around the calf's neck like that's where it belonged. I jerked the slack, pitched the rope forward out of the way, grabbed the horn in my right hand, laid my left on Fooler's neck (which was his signal to slam on the brakes), and bailed off.

Old Fooler stopped with his hindquarters low and his hind feet tucked way up under him. I hit the ground running and got there just as the calf came down hard on his side. There had been a sudden stop on the calf's end of that rope. Just as I reached him he got up. It was a good thing because the rule says, *You have to have daylight under a calf's belly before you throw and tie.* I caught him just right as Old Fooler was pulling him toward me with a tight rope. I picked up the calf's right foreleg, lifted, pushed, and kneed him in the belly all at the same time. Over and down he went. I jumped over, holding that foreleg up straight next to my face, pulled the piggin' string out of my mouth, and latched the small loop over the foreleg just below the ankle. I pitched it out of the way while I reached back and gathered up the two hind legs. I had my right knee under those legs, helping to hold. I got the three legs bunched together and held them with my left hand. With my right I gathered up the piggin' string about sixteen inches from the leg and made my first wrap. It's the first wrap that holds, so I made it tight. Then I made two more fast wraps and jerked a hooey in the rope and threw my hands out, signaling the timers to stop the clock.

"Nice job, Dusty," old Sy was saying. "Just a minute, folks, and we will give you the official time."

I walked back to Old Fooler where he still held the rope tight and mounted him. I spurred him forward to take the slack out of the rope. A cowboy took the loop from around the calf's neck and turned him over. I held my breath but the tie stayed. Then the judge waved to the timers that the tie was okay. The arena hands took my piggin' string off the calf and handed it back to me. I turned and rode for the gate out of the arena, hoping and praying every step that Old Fooler wouldn't change his mind at the last minute.

"Here it is, folks," said Sy Wheeler, "the best time of the day—sixteen-two."

It was a nice thing to hear. I rode on out and turned around to watch the rest of the roping. I still had a long way to go before I won the money.

There were five ropers left to go. Well, one missed, one got tangled up in the rope, two of them tied in slow time.

There was only one roper left. I heard his name called, Walter Hall from Canadian, Texas. I almost swallowed my dry tongue. There is always a bunch of good rodeo hands from that part of the country. This kid, maybe eighteen or nineteen, rode in the arena. He had a high-powered buckskin quarter horse. His equipment was the best. I could tell he was one of them rich ranch kids that had never done anything but practice roping. He rode in there, turned around, and before I knew it he had signaled the chute man and was out of there after his calf. He had crowded the barrier just right—touching it as it broke. He rode out there with a little old bitty loop that wouldn't fit around a wild steer's horns in a hundred years, but it sure did fit around that calf's neck. He got off and threw that calf and tied him so damn fast you couldn't hardly see it.

I turned to Coy and said, "There went my first money. There has always got to be a smart-aleck kid around."

"Yeah," said Coy, not feeling too good because I had at least beat him.

Sy Wheeler damn near choked when he made the announcement: "Twelve point four, folks. The best time of the day."

Well, I had got second money, and that wasn't much to kick about. Besides, for once I had beat old Coy Beasly. Then, too, I was not only relieved but kind of proud about Old Fooler.

The saddle-bronc riding came next, and then the announcer yelled for all cowboys to get ready for the wild-cow milking.

Now, at most rodeos they line up two cowboys on horses as a team and turn a wild cow loose. After she passes a line out in front, the cowboys are allowed to rope and milk her. One cowboy will rope, the other will jump down and mug her. The roper will take a coke bottle and squeeze just enough milk in it so it will barely pour, then race back to the judge.

At Hi Lo, they do it different, though. It's a lot more reckless and a lot more fun. They take the whole herd down to one end of the arena and the ropers all line up at the other end. There is only one loop allowed, so there is no use for the mugger to be horseback. He can wait out there afoot and get to his cow faster that way through this tangle of cows, ropes, and scared horses.

Wrangler stood there waiting, rubbing his hands together above his little round belly. I built a big loop and got all set. I had picked out two head of cows from the bunch that was horned. I knew that a cow stands a lot better if she's roped around the horns. She don't choke so bad.

Sy said, "Get ready."

The cowboys at the other end had started the whole herd right at us as fast as they could make them move. I only know of two other places in the country where they hold a wild-cow milking like this—Cimarron, New Mexico, and Calgary, Canada.

The whistle blew and the cowboys all spurred out, trying to be first. I knew a lot of loops would be wasted right quick, so kind of easy-like I loped Old Fooler out and worked in beside the cow with the horns. It was plumb easy. I had her! Wrangler was right there and mugged her. She stood like a Jersey milk cow. I ran around behind her and took her tail in my mouth to keep it out of the way while I milked. It wasn't any too tasty, but I didn't have time to think about it. I squeezed them tits a couple of times and got some milk in the bottle. Then I ran back to Old Fooler, stepped on, and rode him up, giving Wrangler slack in the rope. The rule said, *The rope has to be removed from the cow.*

Wrangler jerked the loop off and yelled, "Ride, you bastard, ride!"

I did. We had beat the second best by a full fifteen seconds. It was a very nice feeling, but I couldn't help wondering what in the hell had come over Old Fooler. I was feeling about half let down because I'd expected him to blow up all along. Otherwise I felt as good as a fat hog with his belly in the mud and his back in the sunshine as I rode toward the gate out of the arena. Then I glanced up in the stands for no particular reason, and there set Jim Ed Love, beaming and waving down at me like a preacher at a tent meeting.

I forgot for a minute that me and Wrangler had gathered in two second places and a first already. I forgot everything except how I would like to bash that grinning face in. How could that bastard still act friendly after the cussing we had give him while we was quitting his outfit for good? It beat me.

The arena hands set three oil barrels in a triangle for the girls' barrel race. Then a bunch of young girls and women ran their horses around them one at a time against the clock. It was a popular event. Nineteen seconds flat won it, and everybody clapped real loud.

The horse races went off pretty fast, and then the final event came up. The brahma-bull riding. There was a feller dressed up like a clown, and he was out there cracking jokes and doing crazy tricks, keeping the crowd laughing. When one of those bulls unloaded a rider, that clown was right in the bull's face, luring him away. He saved lots of lives and took lots of chances with his own life doing it.

A rodeo bull is twice as big as one of those faced by a Spanish bullfighter. He is just as quick and charges with his eyes open instead of shut. He will turn like a cat and is completely unpredictable. That clown, or bullfighter as the rodeo hands call him, makes a joke out of the whole thing, but he faces a lot more danger than those tordors or whatever they call them.

Old Wrangler drew a twisting, running bull that threw him the first four or five seconds. The bull went for him, and the clown ran up and put his hand on the bull's forehead. He ran along in front of him like that, cutting up to beat hell. Then he sidestepped and let the bull go by. The crowd got a big kick out of this, and you could hear them holding their breath and then gasping all at the same time. Then the show was over for the day.

But the Fourth of July still had a lot of hours to go!

Mary and Kate came over and grabbed me and Wrangler around the necks, telling us what a hell of a fine job we had done. It made a feller feel right proud. We walked over and got our money and then stood around drinking beer while the crowd cleared out. Some of the hands that hadn't made any spotted our free beer and it wasn't long till it was gone.

Shorty Wilson came over and said, "Well, you got away with it today, Dusty, but you'll never make it through tomorrow."

"Make what?" I asked.

"Why, that horse, that's what. He'll come unwound tomorrow for sure."

"How do you know all this?" I said.

"I been talking to Jim Ed."

"To hell with Jim Ed," I said.

Shorty saw this conversation was making me mad, so he changed the subject. "Where you staying?" he asked.

"Hell's fire, I don't know," I said, taking a drink out of the last can of beer. "Reckon we'll get a motel room."

"Can't," said Shorty. "They're all full. Listen," he said, "you need a place to put your horse. Come on down to my outfit. I've already let all the beds out, but seein' as how you've got bedrolls you can sleep in the barn. It's better than nothing."

I looked at Mary. I called her off and said, "You feel like another night in a bedroll?"

"Why, honey," she said, looking up at me like a suckling calf at its mama, "anything that suits you—"

"Okay," I said.

I went back to Shorty and said, "Thanks, Shorty, we'll take you up on it."

I knew Shorty still figured he was going to get Old Fooler for the dog-food maker. He was sure as hell right, too, but I was going to hold out for a little more money now. We loaded up Old Fooler and took him out to the edge of town and turned him loose in Shorty's corral. Then we headed for town to get something to drink.

There is a lot of dust around a rodeo arena, and it has a tendency to make a feller choke up and his eyes water. They had several places in Hi Lo just made to cure such ailments—the best one being the Wild Cat Saloon.

There was people of all kinds in this place—businessmen getting in a few extra licks with their year-around customers and trying to latch on to some new ones. Ranchers stood around talking about cow prices and grass conditions. The working cowboys was drinking like they invented it, and beginning to brag. The jukebox was going full blast, and every now and then somebody would jump up and go to yelling and dancing. One of them was old Wrangler.

We had a lot of talk about different things that happened at the show, and finally everybody got sure-enough drunk and settled down to some real honest-to-God deep-down bragging!

There was old Sowbelly who was still griping about his bad draw on his horse. He kept saying as how he could ride anything that walked, crawled, or flew. Some of the others agreed that he was right but they could do him one better. They could do all that and roll a cigarette at the same time.

It just kept getting worse until I joined in. I didn't brag on me or Wrangler because I had a plan. I got to telling those bronc riders that I didn't think there was too many good riders left around and

I went on to say, "Hell, my ropin' horse can throw any rider I saw out there today."

Well, I had so many bets called before I knew what happened that I had to put a limit on it. I took on Sowbelly and two more boys at twenty-five apiece. Then we asked L. C. if it would be all right if we put on this special exhibition just after the calf roping the next day.

He said sure. Then he called me off to the side and said, "Dusty, what in the hell is the matter with you—matching that ropin' horse against three good riders in a row?"

"It's like I always said, L. C., I was just plain dumb to start with, and have got stupider since. But here's fifty more says I am right."

L. C. reached for his money and then stopped. "Naw," he said, "you know somethin' I don't. That old horse is too bad scarred up."

There was a big dance after the show down at the schoolhouse. We didn't make it, though. We changed over from beer to whiskey, and the girls got off on screwdrivers again. We held a little dance of our own in the Wild Cat, and besides, I still was getting bets that Old Fooler couldn't down three top-notch riders in a row.

Finally the bar closed and we went down to Shorty's barn and crawled into our bedrolls. We was tired but happy.

FOURTEEN

The second day there was a bigger crowd than ever. We got the grand entry and all over with pretty fast. Wrangler made a fair ride on a little sorrel mare called Twist. But I didn't believe he was in the money. I was the third roper out. I drew a little blue calf that ran like a scared rabbit. Old Fooler built right on top of him. It was an easy loop. I got down and took him even quicker than I had the day before. But I made a bobble on my tie, and the announcer called the time at seventeen point one. I had a hell of a lot of sweating to go through—almost two dozen ropers to come.

Well, when it was all over I had taken third money. The kid that had beat me out of first money the day before missed his loop, but another tied one in thirteen-five. Coy Beasly took first in the two-day average, and I had second. It was the best I had done in six or seven years. Our luck was sure running.

Then Sy Wheeler made the special announcement. "Folks, we have got a little bonus for you. Something a little out of the ordinary. You just saw Dusty Jones win third in the day money and second in the two-day average on that bald-faced roan called Old Fooler. Well, now get this, folks. He has bet a considerable sum of money that this very ropin' horse can throw three good bronc riders one right after the other."

I could hear the crowd buzzing and heads was turning all over the place.

Sowbelly, Doak Andrews, and Sandy Washam was all lined up over at the bucking chutes ready to ride. L. C. yelled for me to bring Old Fooler on over and get the show on the road.

Sowbelly was the best rider of the three, so he was going to go first. I led Old Fooler into the bucking chute from out in the arena. He acted real at gentle—like I was fixing to turn him out to pasture. Sowbelly threw his a saddle on him and cinched her up tight. Old Fooler just stood there half asleep, like he had done me the first time I ever saddled him up.

Sy Wheeler was saying, "Now, folks, this has to be a contest ride just like any other rodeo horse."

I was a little scared, but when I heard this I got my confidence back. To make a contest ride a feller has got to come out of that chute with his spurs in the horse's shoulder and keep spurring all the time. He has to keep that right hand up so it don't touch the saddle anywhere.

All of a sudden I was wishing I had more money to bet. Hell, there had been plenty of times I couldn't ride the old bastard pulling all the leather there was on the saddle.

They got the rigging ready, and Sowbelly crawled up over the chute and got set in the saddle. He tested the length of the rein to be sure it wasn't so short he would get pulled off over the horse's head when it went down. If it was too long he wouldn't have any control either. That rein had to be just right.

When he was all set, Sowbelly looked around grinning and said, "Turn this plow horse out of here."

Well, me and Wrangler opened the gate, and I can guarantee the world that there wasn't anybody there disappointed except maybe Sowbelly. Old Fooler hung up just a second, then he felt the spurs in his shoulder, and he tucked his head down between his front legs and jumped about ten feet right straight out into the arena. I'm pretty sure Sowbelly never saw anything but the top of Old Fooler's mane after that.

It was all very familiar. Old Fooler flew way out and sucked back and Sowbelly's hat left his head. Then he went up whirling and came down with his head where his rump had been. Sowbelly lost a stirrup. Then he switched back with a long jump, bawling like a castrated bear and kicking with his hind feet. Sowbelly's head snapped back and then he was sailing up into that cool, pure, fresh mountain air looking for a soft place to land.

Old Fooler bucked on down to the other end of the arena, where the pickup men gathered him in. Sowbelly didn't know it, but he had made a damn good ride. The other two boys hit the dirt so fast they didn't even know what happened.

The crowd went wild, and Sy Wheeler kept yelling in the mike, "Folks, that's the damn'dest ropin' horse I ever saw!"

Me and Wrangler ran around collecting our money. I never saw so much money in my whole life. I had every pocket full and it was still pouring in.

L. C. came over and wanted to buy Old Fooler for his bucking string.

"No," I said, "L. C., that is too good for the son of a bitch. You don't know what all he has done to me. I am goin' to let Shorty Wilson have him, providin' he will sign a paper guaranteein' to sell him to the dog-meat company."

A big crowd gathered around wanting to know about this horse. Now, no matter what kind of horse you got (he may be a combination roping horse and a champion bucker), you never want to mention how fast he is. Somebody will call you on it.

Old Ed Foster said he would bet me all I could raise that his black five-year-old stallion could outrun Old Fooler for a half mile.

I said, "Make it a one-mile race and you've got a bet."

Wrangler called me off and said, "Dusty, you have matched a race with a racehorse."

"I don't care," I said. "Remember how Old Fooler caught that coyote? Why, he can run like a turpentined greyhound."

"By God, that's right!" Wrangler said, and commenced counting his money, getting ready to bet.

I said, "Wrangler, our luck is running. Look at all we have made. If we can win this race—which you know damn well we can—we won't have to put up with fellers like Jim Ed Love any longer. We can buy a little outfit of our own or just go over to Santa Fe and lay around for a year restin' up and livin' high off the hog. Hell's bells," I said, "this ain't the Fourth of July, boy; this is Christmas!"

"That is right," said Wrangler, and went off waving a fistful of money. We bet every dime we had. All our winnings and damn near a year's wages.

Sy Wheeler told the folks about the matched race that would be held immediately after the final event.

I saddled Old Fooler up and led him around till he got any bucking ideas out of his head. Then I got on him, talking soft.

"Fooler," I said, "after all you have done to me I am goin' to make you a deal. Now, listen close, Fooler. You win this race and I will sell you to L. C. All you will have to do then is eat and drink and sleep. On weekends you can come out of them chutes and buck for four or five seconds and that is all the work you will ever have to do. Don't you realize, Fooler, that a buckin' horse has got the easiest life there is?"

He didn't act like he was paying much attention, but I knew he heard every word.

"Now," I went on, "if you let me down, Fooler, old Shorty Wilson is just dyin' to take you to Denver to that dog-food outfit."

Well, the show was over. I was so nervous I didn't even go out for the wild-cow milking, my favorite event. I couldn't take any chances on Old Fooler throwing a fit just before the race.

The show was over, but there was still a hell of a lot of the Fourth of July spirit around. Everybody stayed for the race and there was a lot more people trying to get bets down against Old Fooler, but me and Wrangler had run out of money. Mary and Kate bet all they could scrape up and said they knew we would win.

Now, me and Ed Foster had agreed we would ride the horses ourselves. We lined up. The judges got ready, and a big hush came over the crowd. Then the feller shot the gun in the air and around that track we flew! Everybody was yelling and going crazy. Hell, all I had to do was lean over on Old Fooler and he went by that stallion so fast I could smell the hair scorch. We took a big lead and I knew—we was going to gain a lot more before we circled that track twice. It was money in the bank!

Just about the time I had settled down for a winning race and was wondering how in the hell I would ever be able to spend that much money, Old Fooler quit the track. He just sailed out over the rails like it was a little old hump in the ground and took off toward town. I reared back on them reins with all my might. I sawed and pulled back and forth hard as I could but it just didn't do any good. That crazy bastard ran down between a bunch of scattered houses and then headed for the main drag. There wasn't a damn thing I could do but go along.

He hit the pavement at full speed and damn near fell down making the turn. Then he lined out right down the highway with his ears laid back flat against his evil skull.

I was cussing and yelling my throat raw. Tears would have been dripping down my cheeks except we was going so fast the wind was drying them up before they could hardly get out of my eyes. We went through a red light at the intersection like it was a signal to run plumb around the world.

It was a good thing everybody was out at the rodeo grounds or we would probably have had a hell of a horse-and-car wreck. Then I heard this wailing noise coming closer. It was a siren. The louder it blew, the faster Old Fooler ran. They pulled right up beside us and yelled for us to pull over. Red lights was flashing all over that police car.

I yelled back, "If you can pull this son of a bitch over I will give him to you."

They drove along beside us getting madder all the time. Old Fooler fumed off up toward the city light department. There was a fence, made out of double-strength steel, all around it at least ten feet high. Old Fooler ran through an open gate past the plant, and when he came to that big high fence he tried to jump it. Now that Old Fooler horse is quite a jumper, but he ain't no bird. He got about two-thirds up toward the top, and into that fence we crashed. It bent and laid over quite a ways but we didn't make it through.

By the time I got untangled and the world had stopped dodging around, there stood two great big state highway police. They was saying all kinds of things, some of them not very nice. It seems I had run a red light and a broke the speed limit doing it.

I said, "Fellers, I could not help myself. I was just along for the ride. Besides, I didn't know that speed limit took in horses."

They let me know it didn't make any difference if it was a bicycle or a giraffe, a speed limit was a speed limit. Besides, I had failed to pull over to the curb on orders.

I stood around arguing for a while because I didn't have any money to pay a fine. They said we'd have to go see the judge.

About that time some feller working for the light department came running out and wanted to know what I intended to do about his fence.

I said, "My friend, I'll tell you. You ride this horse back to town and I will fix that fence." It kind of set him back and gave me a chance to mount Old Fooler.

Then the police backed up and got into the patrol car, eyeing Old Fooler kind of skittish-like. "Foller us."

"With pleasure," I said.

That goddam animal fox-trotted back to town like a regular parade horse. The crowd was already in town. Some of them had come looking for me, and they was yelling things like, "When are you gonna enter Man o' War in the Kentucky Derby?" and suchlike. Everybody laughed but me. I bet Old Fooler was laughing hardest of all.

The judge charged me with running a red light, avoiding arrest, and speeding in the city limits. There wasn't a thing to do but appeal it over to district court, for I didn't have enough money to buy an all-day sucker.

When it was all over, I rode down to Shorty Wilson's. Him and Wrangler drove up.

Shorty said, "What happened?"

I said, "Nothin' much. We just loped over to check the light plant. Can't take any chances on that red light at the crossing goin' out. Might cause a wreck."

"Oh," he said. "You ready to sell that horse?"

"Hell, no!" I said. "I am goin' to buy me an ax" (then I thought how broke I was) "or rather I'm goin' to steal me an ax and chop this son of a bitch up in little pieces and deliver him to the meat company myself. Hell," I went on, "I doubt if they'll buy him, though. A dog wouldn't eat this horse."

Then I asked Wrangler, who was looking kind of sad and droopy, "Where's the women?"

"They caught a ride back to Hine's Corner. Said for us to be sure and stop by and see 'em again sometime. Seems like they had enough Fourth of July and figgered they had better get back to business."

"Smart girls," I said.

Well, I can say, and not lie an ounce, that we took a lot of kidding that night. It got so I begun to grin a little myself, though, and we was setting in at the Wild Cat signing them IOU slips just as fast as they would let us.

They had moved the dance over to a vacant building about three doors from the Wild Cat Saloon. We moseyed over and the music was going full blast.

Me and Wrangler picked us up a couple of dark-haired girls. They was painted up in the prettiest colors you ever saw. They was sure nice girls, and when we would leave the dance to go down and have a drink they always paid for the first one. Then I would sign another one of them slips. I signed them all over town.

It didn't seem to matter to the girls, Emma and Dora. They was good dancers, but when I asked Dora if she would like to go down to my bedroll she said it was a mighty nice thought but this was her day off. It was three days later before I figured out what she meant.

We had gone back over to the Wild Cat for about the fourteenth time when a bunch of those Diamond-2 hands came in drunk and raising hell.

Old Wrangler was out on the floor doing a jig and yelling when I heard one of them boys say something about that bag of bones that Dusty Jones thought was a racehorse.

"Girls," I said, "things has gone too far." I got up and went over and looked them hands right in the eye and said, "Did I hear anybody here mention my horse?" *By God*, I thought, *I will cuss him all I damn please, but nobody else is going to very long.*

One feller opened his mouth to say something, and I let go and rammed my fist down his throat just as far as I could. A bunch of teeth went along with it. Then I kicked him in the belly and turned around to see if anybody else wanted to cuss my horse. Evidently some of them did, for about four of them cowboys began to beat on me at once. The air was plumb full of fists, and every damn one of them was connecting with me. I would have gone down a dozen times but every time one would hit me on one side and knock me off balance, another would hit me from the other and straighten me up.

Then things got a little better. There was not any way they could get worse. I heard old Wrangler hollering and began to notice that the pressure was easing. Now just because Wrangler's legs is bowed so bad that he looks like he's squatting does not mean he is weak or puny. Far, far from it. He has got arms like a bull's hindquarters, and his neck is thick as a pine stump. He was thumping them cowboys in the belly, then kicking them in the face when they doubled over.

We was beginning to see daylight and I had got to where I could actually take aim again when those same state police hit the door blowing whistles and pulling guns. It took them quite a while to get things sorted out, and one of them had to give orders from the floor. He had run in between me and the feller who I had first hit in the mouth. This feller was swinging one of them long, get-even punches, and it caught the policeman in the side of the head and down he went. The other one started shooting in the air. Things gradually died down some.

When the policeman saw it was me he said, "You again?" He put the handcuffs on me so fast I didn't have time to salute.

Wrangler was still jumping around swinging and kicking and snorting through his nose—plumb loco. The other cop got up off the floor and hit him under the ear with a pistol barrel. Poor old Wrangler lost all his interest in the fight right then and there. While they was arresting us, the Diamond-2 boys hightailed it out of there and left town.

They took me and Wrangler over to the county jail and threw

us in. It was a long night. It was hot and my nerves was frazzled. I couldn't sleep. Besides, no matter which way I turned there was sore spots and my face was swelled up like a bloated cow's belly. One eye was tight shut. Wrangler was not in much better shape.

About nine o'clock in the morning the jailer came around and fed us some oatmeal and prunes with two cold biscuits and a cup of week-old coffee.

I said to Wrangler, having a hell of a time working my sore jaw, "Wrangler, we are in a hell of a fix. They will have every charge in the book against us and we owe money all over town. What in the hell are we goin' to do? If we don't pay this fine we will have to lay it out in jail."

Wrangler did not give me much satisfaction. He grunted and rubbed one of his swelled-up fists. I was aching all over, inside and out.

The Fourth of July was sure enough over.

We groaned and worried for what seemed like a month. About ten o'clock the jailer came back and took us down before the judge.

I started right in. "We ain't got no money, Judge," I said. "We'll just have to lay it out."

After that horse race yesterday I would have stayed in jail the rest of my life before I would have asked one of these Hi Lo citizens for bail.

The judge didn't pay any attention to me. He picked up the phone, leaving us to stand there twitching and worrying. He called the bank and asked for Mr. Salter, the vice president. Then he put the phone down and smiled at us. That is the first time in my life I ever had a judge smile at me. I looked down at my boots to see if there was any cowshit on them.

Then old Salter walked in and laid a stack of little papers out on the judge's desk. It was that bunch of IOUs I had signed. Even with my sick and bloodshot eyes I could see my name wrote there.

Well, I thought, *they are going to send me to the penitentiary for life.* I could just see me and Wrangler using that big sledgehammer and making little rocks out of big ones till we was so old we couldn't lift our arms no more. Then I could see them standing us up against the wall and shooting us full of holes.

I'll be damned if old Salter wasn't grinning. Maybe the same thoughts had occurred to him.

Salter said, "Boys, you are sure lucky to be working for a man like Jim Ed Love."

Then I remembered Jim Ed was a director in his bank.

"Yes, you sure are," the judge said, still smiling.

I remembered something else. Jim Ed was county chairman of the same party that had elected the judge.

I didn't say a thing.

Salter went on, "Jim Ed has picked up and paid all these IOUs. He has paid your fines here, too, and said he was glad to see you boys had a good Fourth of July, but to get on back to the ranch now just as soon as you could. He has a new string of broncs ready for you to top out."

I still didn't say a thing. I couldn't.

"Shorty Wilson is waiting outside with your pickup loaded and full of gas, all ready to go," Salter finished.

Me and Wrangler swallowed back that day-old whiskey and walked out into the dazzling sunshine, as them town fellers say.

Shorty had unloaded Old Fooler and was writing out a check. I went around and opened the end gate and Old Fooler jumped in.

"What's the matter?" said Shorty. "What you loading that horse up for?"

"If I am goin' to have to worry about Jim Ed, I might as well worry about this son of a bitch too," I said, and climbed in the pickup and took off, leaving Shorty standing there waving that check.

We drove out of town just as fast as we could without breaking the speed limit. Pretty soon we was out on the open road. Wrangler hunkered down in the seat so only the top of his head was showing. In a little while we was getting ready to pass Hine's Corner, and I remembered the girls had asked us to stop by. I scrooched down just as low as I could and still see out over the radiator and really pushed down on the foot-feed.

Just when it looked like we would get by without being seen, that goddam bell started ringing again and Old Fooler went to kicking and squealing. I felt like I was naked in church.

I had forgot about the bell, but I wasn't going to stop till we was well out in the country. Pretty soon Old Fooler stopped kicking and went to nickering, keeping pretty good time with that bell.

I wheeled off on that country road. Them bumps sure felt good. I never wanted to hear of another drink of whiskey as long as I lived, and I was sure glad it was a full year till another Fourth of July.

"Wrangler," I said.

He grunted.

"Jim Ed ain't such a bad feller after all. He feeds good, don't he?"

Wrangler grunted.

"There ain't but one windmill on his outfit, and he feeds good," I repeated.

He grunted a little louder, almost talking.

"He don't never interfere and try to tell a man how to break out a string of broncs. All he wants is results. Ain't that right?" I said.

Wrangler sat up a little and said, "Dusty."

"Yeah?"

"You know what a bronc rider is?"

"What?" I asked.

"It's a cowboy with his brains kicked out."

"I reckon you're right," I said.